Degenerescence

By James Chapman

Our Plague: A Film from New York

The Walls Collide as You Expand, Dwarf Maple

Glass: Pray the Electrons Back to Sand

In Candyland It's Cool to Feed on Your Friends

Daughter! I Forbid Your Recurring Dream!

Stet

How Is This Going to Continue?

Degenerescence

James Chapman

fugue state press
new york

ISBN 978-1-879193-18-5

Library of Congress Control Number 2008909076

Cover photo: J. Chapman

Excerpts of *Degenerescence*
have appeared in some anthologies:
Avant Garde for the New Millennium (Raw Dog
Screaming Press, ed. Forrest Armstrong) and
Hatter Bones (Evil Nerd Empire, ed. Paul Jessup);
some magazines:
*Word Riot, Dogmatika, nth position, Mud Luscious,
Subtle Tea, Olympus Found;*
and some blogs:
W.B. Keckler's *Joe Brainard's Pyjamas*
(joebrainardspyjamas.blogspot.com) and
Tim Miller's *House of the Sun*
(houseofthesun.org).

Printed in the United States of America.

Fugue State Press
PO Box 80, Cooper Station
New York NY 10276

www.fuguestatepress.com

Contact the author directly:
jim@fuguestatepress.com

to randie

Degenerescence

I will sing the song of the song, the song of the song.

I will sing the song with the beautiful arms, the song with the beautiful feet, the song with the well-proportioned sword, the mighty song, the song that lives in the garden.

I will sing until SONG comes to me. SONG will teach me the song of the song, the song of the song.

Now if the song is come. Now what do I say to the song?

If the song is come, if the song lets me sing, I will break hilltops, I will burn stone, I will praise the song. I will sacrifice my legs, I will sacrifice my chin and forehead, I will praise the song. I will thank the song, I will lacerate my body. I will beg the song to remain, until the entire song is sung.

Now if the song never will come all my life, if the song will not come. Now what will I say?

I will dress in flax-cloth, I will declare my self as "singer."

I will put ointment on my forehead, I will praise my self.

I will blame all other singers. I will avoid water, I will avoid purification rites. I will not listen, I will not listen!

I know the song will never come. I know. The song will never permit me to sing. I will live as "singer who does not sing."

In the daytime I will praise my former singing, I will scoff, I will make a show of eating soft sakir plants, I will drink matta like one who can sing, I will drink matta like one who is praised for his singing.

At night I will smear honey into my eyes, I will refuse to look. I will fill my mouth with burning leaves. I will refuse to sing, I will refuse to attempt to sing, I will refuse to sing!

May the song appear to me. May SONG please appear to me. Do not spurn me. Do not forget me.

I will give six hundred white goats, I will give twelve thousand baskets of fish, I will eat only a single root. Do not. Do not forsake me.

I will lay out silk clothing for even the mosquito. I will build a brick house for every flea. I will honor every created creature of your island, WOE, every piece of moving and unmoving life will I honor. Do not. Do not forsake me.

I will not sing falsely. I promise it.

I will not sing impurely. I promise it.

I will purify my mouth.

I will wash my mouth with nothing. Not with water or herbs or air or sunlight or spoken spells or musical spells or sour juice. The mouth is washed with nothing, to remove words and names of things.

I will wash my mouth with nothing, to remove words and names of things.

SONG avoids me still, because my mouth is surrounded by gods contending, my mouth needs to be washed.

SONG avoids me still, because my mouth speaks abstract words, my mouth needs to be washed.

My mouth has talked, my mouth has talked like a Briton who writes words, my mouth has spoken names of things that are not things, my mouth has named gods that only live in their names. My mouth needs to be washed.

My mouth needs to be washed, and then to

wait, and to not speak.

The first word a cleansed mouth speaks,
that will have meaning. Meaning is the soul of the
mouth.

A song comes to the place where meaning
is. A song avoids the place where words live in
filth.

Listen, here is WOE. My mouth is pure.
SONG come to me. I will sing about WOE.
SONG come to me. I will say about WOE.
SONG come to me.

Here is about WOE.

When WOE created the three worlds,
WOE first created this world.

She created the world of named things,
this world, where the mobile life of birds and fish
and women each is animated by a name.

She created the world of named things,
this world, where the immobile life of trees and
plants and stars each is animated by a name.

She created the world of named things, this world, where the unliving life of stones and water and air each is animated by a name.

At the instant she created the world of named things, this world, at that instant the two other worlds became created.

These are: the world of the gods, the world of the names. Thank you WOE.

WOE created the three worlds, in one thousand eight hundred days. Thank you WOE.

WOE tells us: This world is founded on the names of gods, this world is founded on the names of things.

The name is the creation. Thank you WOE.

Speak of fish. Take it in your hands. Fish is brought here by the speech of the name "fish." Speaking the name "fish" enables fish to appear. First fish appears in the mind, then in the hand.

When the prayer is made to luscious fish, the entire prayer is to say: *fish*. Luscious fish will surely appear. If a man sits in his boat, he is hungry, he loves the fish, he asks them. He loves them, he asks, he asks them to arrive, he says: *fish*.

He speaks while thinking the thought of luscious fish and tasting fish and smelling fish. Fish, they arrive to him. Such a fisher man catches many fish. A fish will love the fisher man who prays well or sings the name of fish and is joyful in the presence of fish.

The fish in the hand, it is the same as the name of "fish." The name "fish" calls a god. A god is present in any fish, a god is present in all fish. This god has the name FISH, the name of the god is FISH.

Call to a fish and catch a fish, call "fish" and you are speaking to FISH. If FISH loves you, then a fish will appear, to feed your stomach.

The fish in your hand, it is destroyed of its life. The fish struggles. The fish dies in darkness. The fish says: My destroyed ocean, my destroyed sky.

My destroyed ocean, I have been struck down. I lived like silver clouds, I lived like rain water in the sun, I lived like the eyes of the king, the silver eyes of the wife of the king. Now I am on an unfamiliar path. Now I follow a dark path.

That is what the fish says.

FISH speaks to the fish, saying the name "fish, fish."

The fish calms. The destroyed fish calms. The god FISH has said "fish, fish." So the fish knows about the ocean, that the ocean will still live. So the fish knows about the sky, that the sky will still live.

We thank FISH, also we thank the fish, before we eat our fish. We name: "fish, fish." We eat with the name, we eat using the name. We eat with the god, we eat using the god. We eat the fish. The three worlds have given us our food.

In the present, WOE lives with us in this world, in this world. She plays with us and we are permitted to see her without fear, in this world.

Before the past, before the three worlds, before the time of the past, in the distant years, in the remote times, prior to our world, prior to the loss of our language, prior to the silence, prior to the attempt to sing, prior to the creation of our Briton names, prior to the creation of our Europa names, in the years of the remote times, persons ate what was necessary, persons could taste the taste of bread.

In that time there was WOE and there were seven daughters of WOE. Before WOE sailed for another world, before WOE lost the ability to speak, before WOE was old, before WOE gained her enlightenment, before WOE lost her energy, when WOE was young, when WOE was capable of everything except the exercise of wisdom, at that time there was a tree growing at the place the sun sets, it was called the mist-tree.

Before the day of the mist-tree, before the water that came from the mist-tree, before the earth that lived under the mist-tree, before the sun that rose up behind the mist-tree, in the remote time before the remote time, in the distant past before the distant past, WOE was present at the destruction of the previous world, the previous world.

WOE tells us of the creatures of the

previous world.

They were formed of rock, they were
formed of glass, they were formed of ice, they
were creatures of busyness, they spoke loudly,
they laughed, they injured WOE, they accused
WOE, they mocked WOE.

These creatures, they were created by a
naming, as we are. They lost their names in that
world, therefore they had no gods to themselves.

The gods in that world only slid in and out
of words. The gods in that world did not stay
within any word.

In that world, no word was a name.

In that world, you would not say "fish."
You would speak around the fish. You would say:
Cook the one that lives wet.

In our world, the god of each thing is the
weight of that thing. When you lift with your
hand a stone, the weight you feel, that is STONE,
the god. In the previous world, sadness was the
weight, instead of the god of the name. Sadness
kept creatures sticking to the earth.

All creatures in that world injured all other
creatures, and WOE was injured most of all.
Sadness made weight, confusion made movement,
despair brought the rain, torpor brought sleep,
fear was the sun.

The creatures of that world, they began
their existence with words. Then those creatures
felt their words grow thick. Each word became
full of filth. Each word carried a thousand words.
Each word was fat like a fearful anti-god.

The creatures of that world grew afraid.
They lived in blackness. They cried harshly.
Lamentation was all their world. Their words had
grown thick, their words were full of filth.

They poured their wine into the dirt. They
threw their grain into the river. They allowed
their goats to run away.

Their king was chased by goats. Their
dwellings were burnt with fire. Their babies were
deprived of milk. Their women were deprived of
water. Their men were deprived of weapons.

Creatures of that world, they fought each

other as enemies. They fought with their hands.
They wept as they fought. They pleaded with
each other. They begged for a god, they begged
for a name.

As if they were human, creatures perished
in despair. As if they were human, they thought
foolish thoughts. In the destroyed house, they said
without words: *My beauty is still with me.* In the
destroyed city, they said without words: *The fault
is with the others.* In the flames, they said without
words: *Where is my bright neck-chain and my amulet
of lapis lazuli?*

Because there were no clear words remaining for food, because there was no god to speak
"food" to, because there was no god FOOD,
because there was no word "food," the food grew
hungry. The food did not remember to grow. The
grain turned to worms that shifted in the light,
the grain turned to stones that shifted in the light,
the grain was worms and it was stones.

There was no clear word for fear, therefore
the creatures ran without knowing what they felt.
They ran like cattle from the knife, they ran like
cattle from death. But they could also not see
death. Death had no clear word. They could not

remember death, they could not remember fear, they ran like cattle from the knife.

Dogs walked through the city, the dogs were happy, pigs walked through the city, the pigs were full of joy. The animals found food and drink, food and drink were every place, only the words had been lost.

The creatures mourned, they feared each other, they struggled for words, they tried to sing, they wept, they sang alone: May we understand. May there be food upon the ground. May there be rainwater for drinking. May we remember. May our lives return to us. May the dark spot where honey was, be brightened. May the dark place where grapes were, be brightened. May the order of our laws return to us. May our former terrifying king, our slaughtering king, our ignorant king, be returned to his justice-throne to rule over us. May our king's henchmen be allowed again to kidnap and kill throughout the city, as before. May persons eat. May the city be normal. May there be no change. May there be no collapse. May there be no degeneration. May there be no change. May there be no change.

This is what the creatures sang. Only there

was no word to sing for any of these. There was no word to sing for honey, rainwater, grapes or king.

WOE, whose name was not yet named, WOE walked through this world, WOE saw these things.

She was without a name, therefore without body. When the named things of that world slowly lost their names, when the named creatures of that world slowly lost their names, she alone was apart, who had never been named. When the things of that world became a fluid mass, when the creatures of that world became a fluid mass, she alone was apart.

She watched the sky flow down into the mountain.

She watched the mountain flatten and enter the sea.

She watched the sea stretch itself into the long unmoving plain.

She walked thousands of miles.

Sun and moon did not remain, nor fire nor
either one of air or sky. Word did not remain.
Stone did not remain. Bird and person and fish
did not remain. Time did not remain, breath did
not remain. Eyesight did not remain.

On the plain she walked one thousand of
miles. The end of time had come. She walked two
thousand of miles. Falsehood was the same as
what was. She walked three thousand of miles.
Because there were no cows, there was no milk.
She walked four thousand of miles. Because there
was no milk, there were no cows. She walked five
thousand of miles. Meanness, envy, cruelty,
unkindness, flattery, greed, the desire of a creature
that other creatures do a service for it, the desire
of a creature that it impress and amaze other
creatures, the knowing what is evil and then
doing that, hypocrisy, decrepitude, drought, the
loss of vital abilities, the loss of confidence, the
clinging to a false image, the decision of a creature
to scream and cry when it knows it need not make
a sound, the attempt of a creature to gain pity and
sympathy by claims of weakness and need, creature darkness, creature aimlessness, creature
meaninglessness, creature stupidity, creature
aggression, creature weakness, creature forgetfulness, the impotence of the sun to create one more

day, the impotence of the moon to pull one more tide, the impotence of the creatures to retain their gods, the impotence of the gods to continue to love the creatures, these items had degraded the world into a molten plain of nothing. She walked six thousand of miles. Her clothing, which had names in the old world, melted away. Her body, which had not the name of "body," still walked. She walked seven thousand of miles. In all, she walked seven thousand of miles.

The side of the world that contains all gods, it was melted into degradation. The side of the world that contains all words, it was melted into degradation. The side of the world that contains all things, it was melted into degradation. All the three worlds were melted into a plain of nothing. WOE walked seven thousand of miles.

WOE saw the god SKIN was melted until it was empty entirely. It appeared SKIN was made of many creatures. There were creatures coming out of SKIN, melting, the creature who said: *I am beautiful*, he melted, the creature who said: *I ignore every thing I touch*, he melted, the creature who said: *I need you*, he melted, each one came out of SKIN and began to desire, and in desiring he melted, until SKIN was empty. And SKIN appeared as a sack with no inside and no outside.

WOE saw the god named STATUE was melted until it died. Formerly STATUE appeared to support the chipping-out of any statue at all. If STATUE was your friend, you could make statues. WOE saw STATUE melt into several smaller gods. One was called WHY, one was called NOT-CARE, one was called DESTROY-ALL.

WHY melted immediately and left no sign. NOT-CARE did not melt even when it died, it did not change shape until it burned finally and blew away in ashes. DESTROY-ALL stayed alive, it would not melt or die. It moved all across the plain, it grew, it became the sky that was gone, it became the earth that was gone, it became the plain. DESTROY-ALL was the plain, it disappeared in that way, DESTROY-ALL was the melting.

WOE saw every word she ever spoke, she saw them. She saw the word "my," she saw the word "flute," she saw the word "give." She saw every word. The words did not live on the side of

the world where words live. They were on the
plain of nothing and she saw them empty out.

   She saw the word "know." The word
"know" broke open and spilled out. The word
"know" contained many creatures. There was a
creature who could not close his mouth. He spoke,
saying: *Destroy every thing that makes you unsure.*
He melted and died into the plain. There was a
creature with no genitals and no hair, who said:
I am very beautiful. It melted and died into the
plain. There was a creature without the ability to
think or see, who said: *I dwell in all places, I am
every thing.* He melted and died into the plain.
WOE saw "know" empty, it was like a sack with
no inside and no outside. It burned and scattered
ashes until it was gone.

   She saw items or things rise up to praise
themselves. A jar praised itself in its beauty. It
said: My maker, the king of all glass jars, made
me the most great of all glass jars. I was a free gift
of beauty to every future person. I was an expres-
sion of the in-dwelling soul of my maker. I was a
speech of calm and joy to all persons. I was trium-
phant, I smashed all other jars, including my
brothers and sisters. I was the gathered wisdom of
all glass makers. I was more important than the

private life of my creator. I was more important than the private lives of those who looked upon me. I was a blue glass jar. I decreed destiny. I ruined men who yearned to make a jar like me. What liquid I contained was only an offering to me. I had no practical purpose. I was the only true meaning in our empty universe.

That is what the glass jar said. WOE saw the glass jar melt and vanish away. She saw all objects melt and vanish away.

So that nothing was. Only WOE remained. At her command, the plain was black, the plain was red. At her command, flowering trees appeared and vanished. At her command, persons appeared, they appeared, they spoke together.

Nothing was here, a plain of nothing.

WOE played with names. Her command brought a shepherd, a royal prince, a monkey equaling heaven.

Then WOE did not know what to do. So her command brought the three creatures into war against each other.

Then WOE did not know what to do. So her command caused the monkey to defeat the shepherd and the royal prince.

Then WOE did not know what to do. So she made the monkey ascend to heaven on a somersault cloud.

Heaven, cloud, monkey, the corpse of the shepherd, the corpse of the royal prince, the unseen sheep, the unseen kingdom, the unseen ancestors of the three creatures, all these were in front of her. She did not know what to do.

So she said: *Then they melted back into the plain.* They melted back into the plain.

She did not know what to do.

She spoke. She spoke names, she spoke the names.

Without telling a story, she sat and spoke the names. Some names she remembered, some names had never been spoken prior.

She only spoke because she was alone, and there was nothing. She was alone, and there was nothing.

She spoke the names, she did not cease speaking.

She spoke the name of barriers, she spoke the name of copper, she spoke the name of dice, she spoke the name of toy birds, she spoke the name of ocean.

She spoke the name of loyalty, she spoke the name of cow's milk, she spoke the name of sexual intercourse, she spoke the name of dysentery, she spoke the name of stone.

She spoke the name of jewels, she spoke the name of houses, she spoke the name of oxen, she spoke the name of yearning, she spoke the name of charcoal.

She spoke the name of bitterness, she spoke the name of fire, she spoke the name of family, she spoke the name of axes, she spoke the name of judgment.

She spoke the name of youth, she spoke the name of wisdom, she spoke the name of stinging flies, she spoke the name of burrowing flies, she spoke the name of war.

She spoke the name of sun, she spoke the name of planning, she spoke the name of knife-throwing, she spoke the name of laughter, she spoke the name of decay.

She spoke the name of work, she spoke the name of lies, she spoke the name of alcohol, she spoke the name of edible rats, she spoke the name of the three worlds.

She spoke the name of rebellion, she spoke the name of snakes, she spoke the name of sleep, she spoke the name of doorless chambers, she spoke the name of mud.

She spoke the name of tree-shrews, she spoke the name of religious hatred, she spoke the name of flooding, she spoke the name of small-ness, she spoke the name of cremation.

She spoke the name of cobras, she spoke the name of writing, she spoke the name of the two rivers, she spoke the name of altars, she spoke the name of ashes.

She spoke the name of miscegenation, she

spoke the name of faience, she spoke the name of flutes, she spoke the name of mussels, she spoke the name of gold.

She spoke the name of terracotta, she spoke the name of yoni worship, she spoke the name of avoidance, she spoke the name of hymns, she spoke the name of bamboo.

She spoke the name of astrologers, she spoke the name of fishnets, she spoke the name of moneylending, she spoke the name of lightning, she spoke the name of thorns.

She spoke the name of pillars, she spoke the name of clapping, she spoke the name of boats, she spoke the name of murder, she spoke the name of drinking-water.

She spoke. She spoke. She spoke for one thousand and eight hundred days.

She stopped speaking.

She looked at her body. I have breasts, she said, I have glorious arms, I have long legs, I have glorious genitals, I have long feet.

Because she named these things, they joined to her. I am a body, she said. I am become a body, the body's name is WOE. The body will be called WOE.

She looked up from her body. The rest of the world was in motion around her. The plain of nothing was gone, the plain of nothing was become an ocean, a land, a sky, persons piling up chops of wood, woodcocks eating insects.

She named every thing. She named every way of things.

She mispronounced the name "story" when she spoke it. Therefore "story" did not appear. No person or thing was living in a story, because of the absence of STORY.

She named pain, melodramatic speech, revenge, poetry, ending, beginning, chitchat, also all the other parts of story. All these names lived within STORY, yet STORY did not appear.

Therefore no one made a better speech than one could make. In those ancient times, no person flew through the air. No person did a hundred actions in a row, leading to a final action.

Persons lived and then died in the ancient days. That was not a story.

Within WOE was the word "story." Though she mispronounced the name, she knew the name, she carried it on her back.

WOE walked through the world and looked. She saw every thing and remembered speaking its word. She saw every good and evil thing she had named.

She said the word deterioration, she said the word age, she said the word loss, she said the word forgetfulness, she said the word weakening, she said the word degeneracy, she said the word crumble, she said the word useless. She said the word meaningless, she said the word lonely.

She saw every thing she made.

Every word she spoke, it came to her. She wore every word on her back.

She was clad in storms, in blood, in fear, in terror, in destruction. Creator of the world, she created destruction, she created decay.

The bright desert, it came from her mouth. The empty dream, it came from her mouth. The fraudulent love affair, it came from her mouth. The struggle to know, it came from her mouth. The unfulfilled desire for immortality, it came from her mouth. The refusal to understand truth, it came from her mouth. The desire to be normal, it came from her mouth.

WOE created the universe, for what reason? She has created the universe, and for what reason? WOE, the woman, created the universe, for what reason?

She spoke the word "reason," she spoke the word "create," she spoke the word "universe." She spoke those names. Do not ask her the reason she created the universe!

She has limbs, she has beautiful limbs, she has a body.

WOE is a woman who gives birth. How can she be a perfect woman? How can she be a perfect being?

Because of WOE, we can see every fish in

the sea, we can see the violet rivers below the earth. Gods give their actual bodies to our food, so the flour and the fish are flavors like sparks of fire. We weep. This is WOE's doing.

Because of her great love, she is perfect. Because of her great resentment, she is perfect. Because of her great injury, she is perfect. Because of her great disregard, she is perfect. Because of her great forgetfulness, she is perfect.

She has limbs, she has beautiful limbs, she has a body. She looks at the world, she is what she sees. She has no body, she is what she sees. She hears the world, she is the eight directions, she has no body, she is the eight directions.

When she sleeps she is only her dreams, she has no body, she has no beautiful body. When she sleeps and does not dream, she is the bliss of dreamless sleep, she has no body, there is no WOE, she is death, she is not here. She is in the words she spoke, she is each word, she is every thing.

WOE in anger at the men of the island, WOE in fear of the men of the island, she withdraws from the company of the men of the island.

In private, she bruises her cheeks, she bruises her buttocks, she bruises her head, she bruises her hips, she bruises her eyes. She places an egg-shaped stone under her tongue, then she gives birth to seven daughters, by naming them.

She will give birth to Opa, which name means *energetic, confused.*

She will give birth to Twick, which name means *dry, strange.*

She will give birth to Glasp, which name means *violent, pained.*

She will give birth to Icic, which name means *betrayed, yearning.*

She will give birth to Dif, which name means *exalted, beautiful.*

She will give birth to Test, which name means *foreign, endless.*

She will give birth to Hit, which name means *words of another.*

She performs the rites of cleansing, to

atone for her daughters. She performs the purification bath, to atone for her daughters. She burns cedar, to atone for her daughters. She burns sandalwood, to atone for her daughters. She undoes the lash of the whip, to atone for her daughters. She undoes the insulting shout, to atone for her daughters. None of her children is ever injured by her tongue, none of her children is slapped on the face by her hand. WOE is perfect and her seven daughters are perfect.

They live together among the white cedars. WOE has created the world, yet only her seven daughters know her. All other persons of her creation ignore her or shun her as a shamed mother, an unmarried mother. She created them, and they treat her as a shamed mother, an unmarried mother.

She speaks, saying: Although I was a human being, I remained alive during all times.

When the moon first rose, I could have died at that time.

When Magellan came like a wave over mankind to destroy the world and make it an island, I was alive then, but I remained alive.

No human can live forever, therefore I will die. Before I die, I will become worse or less good. It is a rule.

When dead, I will move as a ghost among my accomplishments. No one will touch or bother with my accomplishments, so I will be alone.

My accomplishments were seven daughters and several hymns, about three hundred. I failed to have an eighth daughter. I made some flute songs.

I will be dead. I will go to where the dogs lie down, to where the cows lie down, to where the trees lie down, to the place where my grandfather lies, to where persons lie whom I do not know, to the place Magellan lies, to the place our first kings lie, the area of stone where the worthless companions of youth all lie still.

And my accomplishments, they will come to meet me, as if they are elders. They will pass judgment on me. I will have to stand silent, as you do in the presence of an elder. And if I drink water in front of my accomplishments, I will have to avert my face as I drink.

They will tell me this rhetoric:

Having created several daughters and
hymns, having carried buckets of water many
miles for other persons, having sat beside dying
elders and given them the formulas of hope,
having assisted in the death of Magellan, you
have founded a temple in the after life.

However:

Having lost your memory, having lost the
ability to hymn, having failed to birth your eighth
daughter, having lost your energy, having ceased
to speak of real things—trees, water—and begun
to speak in words without gods—"purity,"
"grace"—having lost every amount of beauty you
once had, having attacked the image of your
younger self, having lost even the desire to be
young, having gained in sureness and smugness,
having called yourself wise, having called yourself
enlightened, having treated the young persons of
your island as if they are unformed blobs, having
brought the word "callow" to earth, having ended
your life in complaints, having ended your life in
passive waiting, having ended your life in halluci-
nations of gods and tigers—you have destroyed

the temple you built in the after life.

That is the end of the remarks of the accomplishments.

In the early part of the days of the world, before the moon appeared, in that time the world was inhabited by calm persons. There was very little of constructing gates or mining metals, these things were not needed. The existence of the sky was sufficient, also water was a great gift. Sticks and small things were entertaining and pleasurable.

The king was that person who was most kind and wise. The daylight that rose from the mountain would fill each king. WOE would touch each king in his sleep, WOE would name him by his second name, which was hidden. This name would dominate his first name and join with the name "king" to produce light in the names like the light from the mountain. Any king will shine in the night, this has always been seen.

In the ancient times, the birds with long feathers flew with no audience. They made their flying at night, and nested in day as a secret bird.

In the original time of our island, tigers lived with us on the island. Most such tigers were all white but there were also some blue or bluish tigers, these were more fierce by a small amount of fierceness. To play with tigers was a game for the youth who were tall and swift and also made music.

They (ancient persons) also did not worship or fear any gods, they only spoke those names with fondness, and were calm in their thoughts of gods and words. No rules of speaking were ever thought of, not grammar nor strictures of what could not be said. Each speech spoken was gold.

In the ancient days persons were happy. In the ancient days there were no events. In these ancient days there was no history.

In that time, persons walked in the forest, they looked at trees, they spoke of small things. In that time, persons had no fights. They visited each other's huts and spoke of small things. Ancient persons spoke of food, of rain, of branches of trees, of how the wood burns, of how the sky changes, of how the seasons change, of how persons age.

Ancient persons did not require stories because they did not enjoy danger, suspense, fighting, floods, dramatic shouting, crowd events, war events, wild beasts, vendettas, revenge, sorrow, mourning, death, or love in its painful aspects.

They told stories that would not today seem to be stories.

They wrote these stories into clay, and we still have pieces of them. They tell the story of the man who had his hair cut and spoke to the barber. The man and his barber talk about the pleasures of lanterns, the taste of potato-wine, the red ribbons on the woman who lives nearby. They speak of their dreams. They speak of a white lion. At the end, the man's hair has been cut in an admirable way, the story describes the way of the hair in detail, this is the end of this story.

I who tell this, I tell a story. I was born in a time of stories, I am speaking. Here is what I said to WOE at the time of my death:

WOE of the divine poem, I am dying. Please speak for me.

On the day of the birth of your seven daughters, I gave numerous fat cows and ewes to the flame. Now I am dying, please speak for me.

WOE, timeless creator, who has spoken seven times, who has composed all songs by speaking "song," who has won all footraces by saying "footrace," I am dying, my body is ill. I can not raise my head, I can not step upon my feet.

My lady, who never judges but only accepts, my lady, who never deletes but only adds, my lady, whose fame is growing on the land, whose fame is white like the moon, my lady, who desires to create, who desires to never destroy, save me, save me. Make me well, take my name, take my voice, speak with my name, speak with my voice.

Tell the persons of the island all I should have told them, tell them. Your voice reaches to the outer heaven, tell them how I feel, tell them who I am, tell to them my name.

Fill my sickroom with every person alive, let them listen to me. Give out the cakes and matta, let persons sing, let persons laugh at me, let them toss seeds at my face. I will lie still.

Let them sing the funny songs about me, as I lie helpless. Let them try to make me smile or laugh. I vow I will not smile or laugh, I will not destroy the ceremony.

Take my name. WOE, take the name you gave to me.

Speak for me. Tell my whole life. Tell my life from before I was ever born.

Speak my name, carry the heavy future for me. Take the name out of my mouth and make promises to the gods in my name, in my voice.

Tell the listeners the truth. Tell about the persons I am angry with. You know about me, you have my name.

Tell all the scandals and gossip I know, tell it. Tell cruel things. Imitate the voices of those in the audience who once told me their secrets.

Make the poison leave me.

If you will take my name, then without a

name I can float in my sickbed. The gods of sickness can not adhere to me, I have no name to sicken, I have no name to kill. Without a name I have no past or memory. I have no preference, I have no enemy, I have no way of singing, I have no spirit, I am light, I am without heaviness.

Shout at the listeners. Make them angry. They will walk to you, shouting my name at you. They will stuff your mouth with nettles that burn.

Spit nettles at them. Shout the truth. Make the persons weep.

They will shove torches of fire at your face, they will push torches of fire onto your body. They will shout at you, *Stop this, How dare you take his name. How do you know these things? You know nothing.* They will remember me, they will love me.

The illnesses are terrified. They can not stick to me. The illnesses are horripilated, they must flee, they must go to their own world.

WOE you will put my name back in my mouth again. Now my name is strong.

You have told my story. My name becomes the many events of my life. My name is all events put in one place, in my mouth.

Do this out of love for me. Love me as you love your daughters. Do not let me die, do not let me be forgotten, do not let me disappear entirely.

WOE stayed in her hut among the cedar trees with her seven daughters. She did not come to the village, she did not serve as a priest. I who was ill, she never tended me. She tended her seven daughters. I kept my name, I kept my illness.

That is the end of the statement of the man who died.

The persons who were ill, they died, they stopped moving, they moved only very slowly. They spoke no more, they walked no more. Dead persons changed the world by dying, nothing was the same.

WOE never prevented this. She never made a story. She never fought the gods. She bathed in the field of mud. She stayed away and taught her daughters.

She taught Opa. She sprinkled Opa's heart with cold water, and Opa's eyes came awake, and WOE taught her.

WOE taught Opa that water of the river is cold. WOE taught Opa that flesh of many creatures is beautiful. WOE taught Opa that the world is hollow inside and inhabited with creatures within its inner surfaces, and these creatures are kind.

WOE taught Opa that if she speaks the truth with great energy, she will be soon married, she will be attractive and will easily be married.

Opa went out of the place of the cedars. Opa left her home and entered the village. She spoke to all persons she saw, she spoke of what she knew, she spoke with great energy.

No one listened to her words. She sat in the dirt. No one offered her food, she sat in the dirt and was hungry. No one gave her to drink, she lay down in the dirt and waited for five years.

During these five years Opa died, without

any person ever noticing her or speaking to her.

Upon her death, Opa returned to the hut of her mother, and was unable to speak.

Opa's six sisters see Opa killed, they scream. They scream without throats. They see they will be born and die. They are in sorrow. They are like birds who have been caught in a bag.

Being born, then dying, this is a story. To be trapped in a story, this is the worst story.

WOE grieved at the death of her beautiful daughter. WOE kept Opa with her, and fed her and gave her to drink, and though Opa was dead, WOE did not forget her. Opa remained within the hut, Opa could whisper, she could move a little, she did not decay altogether or die like one who is dead.

Opa sat in the hut, she watched a cat with her eyes. The cat was young, it contained the fire, it hunted a bird feather, it killed a bird feather, it was victorious. It sat still. It suddenly ran out of the hut.

Opa was all-fire when she was born. She was all-fire when she appeared to the village. When she waited for five years in the dirt, she was all-fire. Fire when it dies is not fire. Fire is a burning. Opa was burnt.

Every thing Opa looks upon now, it is warmed, it blazes.

She holds a clay cup. She holds the cup and it becomes a red-hot cup. She pours cow milk into a red-hot cup.

Her six sisters watch Opa. Opa is angry, Opa shouts, she drinks the cow milk. She describes the persons of the village. She blames and mocks them. She is unfair, Opa is unfair, the daughter of WOE is unfair and shouts!

Now see, seven sisters. Six are not yet born, one has already died. Opa has been laughed away, she has been ignored away, she has been cursed away. So that her blood has turned to sand, so that her heart has turned to fire, so that her soul has fled to the safety of a black room. But she has spoken her story to the village, so she is certain of herself. She is angry but she has spoken her story.

Each sister will take her turn. Each sister will go to the village, each sister will gather persons in a group at the fire, to speak of herself. Each time, the persons will ignore her messy story, the persons will ignore her senseless story. They will talk among themselves and drink matta and laugh. They will not laugh very much at the sister. They will not notice her. They will laugh about other things.

In the present time, since the destruction and recreation of the world by WOE, in this present time, there has been much mouth laughter. WOE's seven daughters do not engage in the laughter of the mouth. The words of WOE's seven daughters, these words can go into the hearts of even unlistening listeners. Their words can go into a stone and change it. The earth is a stone and it can hear words. It waits for every new word. But it does not hear mouth laughter.

Opa, full of flame, Opa, angry, Opa, aware of her gifts, Opa, aware of her lack of lucid thought, Opa, aware of her beauty, she, Opa, had no knowing or feeling of being in a story. She could not tell a story. Also her sisters could not tell a story.

No man will love them, no man will be their friend. No woman will love them, no woman will be their friend. They can not tell a story.

They will each go into the village. They will each try to speak. They don't know the way to speak to make men and women love them. They are beautiful but they don't know the way to speak.

These are seven children. They could make pots, mend nets, crush roots in a barrel, find plants for eating, make matta, carry water, mend roofs.

Instead they will do these trades:

Opa creates new words.

Twick erases words that are not needed.

Glasp talks to herself about old history.

Icic eats slowly all day and night.

Dif draws pictures of her sleeping dreams.

Test tries to remember another language.

Hit quotes from every person else.

They are daughters of TALK because TALK is the only way love can be altered. Fighting never starts over a drawing, fighting always starts over a word. Each sister has ten thousand gods in her mouth.

Opa is dead, but Twick was born immediately. Twick spoke herself into being. She spoke to Opa, she did homage to her elder sister Opa, she gave Opa words of compassion, she fed honey and dates to Opa.

Twick is born, then she says:

My mother lost her daughter. She needs a daughter.

My mother sees an open leaf. The branch is open, the sky is open.

My mother sees seven trees grow up together into one tree. No birds are in that tree.

All her daughters will die. I will die.

Wind, sound, also a puff of smoke that vanishes. These are the moving, invisible, actual things. They are almost nothing.

My mother, she sees the moving, she sees the invisible.

She needs a daughter. I will visit the village. I will die there. The wind will empty for me. The smoke will vanish for me.

The persons of this village are kind. They laugh about themselves. They know what life is. They make jokes about themselves getting old. They make jokes about themselves and death. They are not cruel persons.

Persons here see beauty in patterns of rust, in mud that is softened by waves of water, also in stone that is worn by waves of water.

Persons here see beauty in broken crystals of sand, also beauty in dead shells.

Persons here see beauty in smell of dead seaweed, the body of a bird, or red feathers scattered across the beach.

Persons here love to see fruit juice rot. The destruction of fruit juice into wine. When the sun sets, stars will appear. The stars are scattered, the stars are confused.

That is what Twick said.

Twick soothed her mother. Twick soothed her elder sister.

She went out among the villagers.

She spoke to them softly. They did not hear her.

She waited five years.

She became ill.

Village, you ignored Twick. May your ears be deprived of bird song. Village, you ignored Twick, you did not listen, you could not understand. May your young men all become priests, and serious, and lose their joy. May your young women gain wisdom at too young an age, and never laugh and never dance. May you lose the use of the few simple words Twick spoke to you.

Fire will consume a reed boat even when it is upon the water. If dates hang from a tree and no bird eats them, they will blacken. If we never taste what is sweet, we walk as if crawling in dirt.

We die, yet we have no enemy. We die and no one has killed us. Twick failed to eat food, because she simplified her words, she purified her mouth. The words for dates, roots, dragonfruit, these words were not with her.

She was small, also she was quiet. Some person could have noticed her. Some person could have come to her. Some person could have listened to her speak. That person, if he heard her speak, he would have fed her. She lived in the words others heard.

She fell ill. The healer did not come to her.

She became crippled. The healer did not come to her.

She became transparent like a leaf. The god LEAF sat on her chest. The god TREE held her.

We die and become corpses, dogs devour our faces, then we lose name. That is how we become free to depart. Dogs came to Twick, but could not smell her flesh. They howled dog words.

Opa and Twick and the other sisters, they were excessive in their wish to please the gods.

The seven sisters all used trances, voices, tongues, poetry.

The seven sisters spoke backwards. They spoke rhythms. They created new words.

The seven sisters, they would repeat a word a thousand times if they felt to.

They screamed and chanted. They over-turned their minds, to speak more fully than a mind will permit.

They yearned, every moment, that the gods would hear them and see them and answer.

Opa spoke, Opa sang, she shouted. She was not heard, she died.

Twick lived and entered the world. She whispered, she purified her mouth, she was not heard, she died.

Twick lay down upon the leaves of the marsh. She did not return to the hut of WOE.

She lay down, in her mouth she held a seed. She held a seed covered under her tongue, so no one could see.

As long as she lay there without speech, no new child could grow or appear in the world.

She did that because she believed one of her younger sisters would destroy the universe.

WOE came to her, in the marsh. WOE touched her, lifted her body. No one in the village ever touched her, but WOE carried her back home.

WOE opened the mouth of Twick, she put her fingers into the mouth, she removed the seed.

WOE said this: My eighth daughter will destroy the world. She will lean over the edge of the world and bend the sea and shear off the sky.

When the world is destroyed, this is what I will sing.

—My daughter Opa, she has lost her body, she can not speak wisely again, she can not love wickedness again, she can not plunder the weak again, she has died.

—My daughter Twick, she has lost her body, she can not climb the mountain again, she can not lay upon the bed of mysteries again, she can not enter the house of the phallus again, she has died.

—My daughter Glasp, she has lost her body, she can not catch me in a trap again, she can not hurt her sisters again, she can not drink pure rainwater again, she has died.

—My daughter Icic, she has lost her body, she can not burn her feet again, she can not walk naked again, she can not cry again, she has died.

—My daughter Dif, she has lost her body, she can not divide her love again, she can not smear herself with dust again, she can not pray to the inexistent gods again, she has died.

—My daughter Test, she has lost her body, she can not dig deep holes again, she can not undermine our faith again, she can not find her way in darkness again, she has died.

—My daughter Hit, she has lost her body, she can not dream of floating weeds again, she can not look at the sunlight again, she can not watch the stars again, she has died.

Because of my last daughter, because of my eighth daughter, because of my unnamed eighth daughter, because of my unborn eighth daughter, my seven daughters have died. Now there will be darkness in the place where my eighth daughter stood. Now the worst day with her. Now the lowliest place with her. Now my eighth daughter will carry her anger knotted in palm-fibre. Now she will be hated by all beings. Now she will carry jars of gall to the rocks. Now she will fetch the ocean in the hollow of her ear. Now she will carry the mountain within her cleft. Now she will disassemble her dreams, so they can be judged.

She is the greatest of women. She is the

work of the gods. She is responsible for all death. She is therefore responsible for all life.

All stones will outlive her. Three pine trees will outlive her. Four fish will outlive her. The pole star will outlive her. Nothing else will outlive her. She will speak the last word spoken.

WOE spoke to her unborn daughters:

Your sister Opa lived and entered the world, her spirit was frightened out of her body, her spirit smashed itself on rock, her spirit threw itself into water. She was cursed by not being spoken to, she was laughed at by not being laughed at, she was injured by neglect, she was destroyed until she was blind, she was destroyed until she could not speak.

Your sister Twick was weak, she had no mouth for speaking. She went into the world and was rained upon, she was blown wind upon, she was burnt in fire, she was drowned in the ocean, she was purified, she was turned into a cloud in the sky for you to see and love.

It would be best for me to produce no more daughters. Instead I should dream. To dream produces no suffering, no yearning, no failures. The dream pictures, the dream words, these go into the air and seek directly to die. They do not become weak, nor do they weep, nor do they remember anything.

None of my daughters will be good. None will become better than my first daughter. My first child was the best of you. She was not good.

Why were they not good? Why were you not good? Why will you be not good in future?

Clumsy, ugly, confused, unable to speak, unable to attract gentlemen, also full of love and yearning that causes all persons to flee you and shun you.

The death of my two daughters has made me weak. How weak I will be after the rejection and destruction and cursing and failure of my next five daughters.

This is what WOE said.

Glasp came into the world, disregarding this speech. She told her sisters of wars and arguments among persons far away. She told her sisters of murder among persons of the far past. Glasp sang war songs during all times of rain, or fog, or enough of darkness.

Glasp knew the feelings of each person who died in each battle in each war. She took their names, she spoke in their names. She was a warrior. She kept her eyes closed, she spoke. She frightened her sisters.

Glasp went to the village and sat down in the ashes in the field where the dead are burned. She sat in the ashes, she spoke of war. She did not know how to tell a story, but she spoke of war. During the first one-year she only drank water. During the second one-year she only breathed air. She was finished then with all her telling. She waited for a third one-year, she stood on one leg and did not breathe.

No god came to her to grant her a boon. She was spattered with blood. She was clawed by wounds. She continued to believe in her own talking. The boy in the cremation yard chased her with ropes, the boy in the cremation yard cast garbage upon her. Dogs told her to die. Birds told her to die.

She bowed her neck to the ground, she ceased to move. No one in the village ever noticed her, except the boy in the cremation yard. He whipped her body with a bamboo pole.

WOE came for her.

WOE said:

Village, my daughters will continue to come to you. My daughters will die here, village, since you will not feed them.

After every word falls out of their mouths, no village will be here.

After every word falls out of their mouths, no world will be here.

Seven daughters will be ghosts. A ghost is a reputation.

Seven daughters will be ghosts. They will not become any better, or worse, or different.

But they will be remembered, forgotten, remembered.

They will be hated, loved, hated.

They will be considered saints, demons, saints.

The man who believes the words "I destroy reputations," the killer of ghosts, he will betray them, he will destroy them, he will erase them.

Then he will be betrayed and destroyed and erased.

My daughters will return. They will return. They will continue to return.

That is what WOE said.

Icic was born. Because of her beauty, because of her passionate voice, because of her knowing of all her own faults, because of hope, Icic was most loved by WOE. Because of her great resemblance to WOE, Icic was most loved by WOE.

Icic was most ugly of the daughters. Her voice was like the split horns of the wild goat in the mountain. Her skin was like the sheet of

66

darkness that ends a sleeping dream. She was too tall to be a girl. Her hair was like the death of a bird in mid-flight. She spoke of friendship ruined, or love ruined, she said too much, she hurt each sister she spoke to. She told her sisters what she felt, she crushed them like malt, she praised nobody, she blamed herself. She was the bowl under the table, she was the bowl on the roof.

Icic went to the village. She shouted, she shouted in the street, in the street beside the place of baking bread. She shouted in the street beside the place of brewing. She disturbed the persons of the village, so that they noticed her. They could not understand what Icic was saying.

She was telling a story, she was telling the story of her older sister Twick, the story of the death of her older sister Twick.

Icic explained: Twick was quiet, Twick died in this village, Twick accepted death as a further quietness.

Twick lived in the village but was not of the village. She was the interior portion of the village, if she only knew. She was the interior portion of the village, if the villagers only knew.

She made the dreams of the village, she made the bravery of the village, she made the purity of the village, she made the desperation of the village. The village caught its fish in her, the village baked its bread in her, the village filled its pots with her, it drank her, it spoke her.

If the village knew this.

The village did not know, so that Twick accepted death, as a further quietness. Part of the island died when Opa died, part of the island died when Twick died, part of the island died when Glasp died.

Icic explained this with shouting. She could not tell a story. The daughters of WOE, they can not tell a story and be understood. When they are beautiful, their beauty prevents them from telling a story. When they are ugly, their ugliness prevents them from telling a story. No person understood Icic.

Icic died as her sisters died, of exposure to rain, also starvation. The neglect of her name did not kill her. The death of a girl is not the death of her name. Therefore the death of her name is not the death of herself. To completely kill her, the village would have to prevent her birth.

WOE came alone to the village, weeping, she wrapped Icic in reed mats, WOE sat beside her body. WOE continued to speak the way Icic spoke. WOE did not want to stop hearing Icic's voice.

WOE, speaking for Icic, spoke of her seven daughters:

The first daughter was never married, she never had a child. She was unprepared for the end of the world. Now she looks into a hollow log and tries to see the universe.

And the second daughter was never married, she never undressed her husband. She was unprepared for the end of the world. Now she eats small stones and weeps.

And the third daughter was never married, she lay open and empty all her life. She was unprepared for the end of the world. Now she argues with herself about past events, unchangeable events.

And the fourth daughter was never married, she never ate at the feast. She was unprepared for the end of the world. Now she picks potatoes, and she cries over the potatoes.

And the fifth daughter was never married, she pretended she needed no one. She was unprepared for the end of the world. Now she sleeps and can not dream.

And the sixth daughter was never married, she said she was pure and strong and beyond the things of earth. She was unprepared for the end of the world. Now she speaks her own language in a false accent, and none understand her, and she believes it is because her ideas are too great.

And the seventh daughter was never married, she said her sisters deserved to be married before her. She was unprepared for the end of the world. Now she only quotes the words of others, no one listens to her because all she says has been said before.

The seven daughters eat food that was rejected by beetles, they walk on paths ignored by slaves, they speak sentences like the stillborn speak, they drink mud, they commune with worms, they groan with pains that are not within their bodies but outside their bodies.

That is what WOE said. WOE took her daughter Icic back home.

Dif, before Dif was born, her hands shook. Upon her birth, Dif saw the clay jug painted with orderly yellow lines in paint. With her foot she kicked the jug so that her foot bled out. She stamped the jug with blood, she painted her nose with blood, she left blood in the dirt of the earth.

She immediately walked to the village, she left blood on the footpath. She spoke to no person, she spoke to all the gods at once. She said they were all one word. No one in the village noticed her speaking, but she did not need their notice.

Dif could see. She saw the faces of persons, so she shouted to the gods. She saw the skin of trees, so she shouted to the gods.

She became dizzy and fell. She shouted, she stood and spun, she fell, she became dizzy and fell. She could not see, then she could see. She swooned out.

Every day she fell and shouted. In her head pained her and she called to the gods for help. The gods did not come.

She became a god, that is what she said. She could not remember being a person. She was not the same as other persons.

She stole food from every person. She ate all night, she took food from the forest, she ate all day. She could not remember eating, she remained hungry, she ate. She stole items from every person and buried them. She grew fat as a water jug.

WOE came to her and she bit WOE on the arm, she bit WOE on the face. WOE brought her home. The household of WOE was ruined by this all-eating daughter. All daughters of WOE had nothing to eat, because Dif ate all there could be.

Dif became a saint by speech. She saw the god CARROT of the word "carrot," she saw the god FISH of the word "fish." Then she saw both have another god in common.

She wondered, she felt, she ate, she wondered, she saw. She called the god of a word a god, like everyone does, but she suddenly spoke: "There is a word called 'god.'"

All her sisters heard her and fell to the floor. Because the god of the word "god" would have to be GOD, the god of every word there is, the god of every thing there is, as it would be the god of all gods.

Dif was then a saint, but was disliked, because of the burden she placed upon words.

No one would come near to her, she was fat, she could not walk, she could not steal food and no one came to feed her.

WOE shouted at Dif, angry. The daughters of WOE shouted at Dif, they were angry.

Dif said, Look at me, I am all the gods, I am truth, I never shout. I am never angry, I am all, I am all.

Finally she was full of spirit and she burst within. She could not speak. She ceased. All gods escaped her at once, and escaped the three worlds, after being trapped in the gigantic Dif.

When she was dead, the gods should have returned to the three worlds. The love of the dear gods and words should have returned. But the gods had now been told of GOD, they were afraid, they were angry with Dif, they were angry with WOE.

WOE's seven daughters, the dead and the unborn daughters, her seven daughters surrounded her and asked her how to live in the world, they asked her what to do. They asked her how she had lived in the world, they asked her what she had done.

They asked her:

Why have you arrived here.

What do you believe in.

What can you swear upon.

What do you care about.

Have you been in love.

What is important to you.

What do you live for.

WOE answered her daughters:

I do not know.

I do not know.

I do not know.

I do not know.

I do not know.

I do not know.

I do not know.

All the daughters, all the dead and unborn daughters, became ill.

Opa became ill because she spoke too much. She fell to the ground and tasted the dust. She wept and hated herself and asked her sisters to kill her. She spoke too much, she became sick, she was sick from her own speech, she stopped from eating.

Twick became ill because she spoke too little. She only said the words necessary to say, so that she forgot how to laugh, so that she forgot how to move forward. Her hands could not hold, there was nothing in her eyes, there was nothing in her mind. She curled up in the mud, then she remained there.

Glasp became ill of opinions. She had an opinion about every item of earth, also every person, also every action. She saw errors every place, and ran and fell. She was sick from knowing the answers, she asked her sisters to help her stop knowing answers. Her teeth chattered, she sat huddled, she sat freezing.

Icic became ill because she spoke her own name. She could see herself at all times and called all other persons by names that came from the word Icic. When she began to believe that the earth was her own belly, she fell face-first and could not rise, she wanted to protect the earth. Her own belly ached.

Dif became ill because of confusion. She was born in a confusion. She saw a bird, she believed it was a path. She saw the sea, she believed it was a wall. She saw the love of a man, she believed it was light. Sunlight was conversely fondness to her or love. She became ill from confusion. She fell sick due to her confusion. She saw her sickness as truth. She became more sick. She fell to the ground. She saw the ground to be a place for her to be born. She then became sick so that she lost her awareness of all things. She dreamed, and her dreams were accurate and not confused.

Test, who was not yet born, was not yet ill. She would become ill because of the attentions of men. The glance of a man was pain to her. She was made for aloneness. She was born to be alone. Her several beauties caused her to wince, shrink back, feel pain, feel ashamed, feel lost, forget her real self, forget aloneness, forget her voice, forget her true appearance. She believed she was truly beautiful, and this made her ill, and this was her illness. She spoke in the manner of a sick person, senseless, without self. She broke with all former habits. She forgot her sisters, she forgot her mother. She saw that she was not beautiful. This made her healthy, but she was ill such that health made her more ill. She fell into the still pond, she lay beneath the water, she was looking up at the water surface. That is a way to see the world without your face in it. She remained underwater and waited.

Hit, who was not yet born, was not yet ill. She would become ill because of voices she heard. She heard voices no one could hear. She heard voices, they told her things no one can understand. They were not her own voice, they were not her own speech. She ceased to be a person. She waited for voices to think for her. She waited for the voices to live for her. She forgot to eat. She supposed the voices would eat when they needed. She forgot to drink, the voices never spoke of water. The voices told her about wives, daughters, wars, machines, music, sorrow, disease. Some of these voices sang. She weakened. No one could remember her name, because she forgot her name, she took all other names, she forgot her name. She was thin. She sat down and could not stand.

The illness of Hit, the illness of Test, these illnesses will be with them when they are born. The illnesses of all the elder sisters, those were also waiting at the time of the birth of them. The death-illness of any person is waiting at the time of the birth of the person.

Opa, Twick, Glasp, Icic, Dif, Test, Hit, all became ill. All the daughters, all the dead daughters, all the unborn daughters were ill. They looked, and they saw no person who would speak their names to them. If the life of their legs failed, and the life of their arms failed, and the life of their chests failed, and the life of their heads failed, and the life of their eyes failed, then they would go off the earth. There would be no breath in their mouths, they would never speak.

They saw they were alone. No one was here to cry out for them. No one was here to moan or lament. If they lost life, no one would give them weeping or mournfulness.

They lived life so as to have no friends. Their mother will leave them alone, their mother WOE will go away to live with birds. Their fathers are unseen like vapor. The stones of the ground saw the dying sisters, the stones did not speak or care.

After the sisters die, no person will know them. No word they spoke will be recalled. After they die, no deed of theirs will have a result. They will pass over the earth without touching it.

They looked at the sky, they imagined themselves in the sky. They looked at the ocean, they imagined the ocean bottom. They described and imagined every thing and every place. But they did not go to those places. They stayed at home.

After they die, their bodies will be distributed by crows. Crows will be made brilliant by the spirit of the muscle meat of these sisters. Such crows will fly in circles, looking for a way out of the sky. Such crows will fly straight up, flying to the sun. Such crows will sing in a thousand voices. But they will not be practical crows, they will forget to eat, they will not live.

The sixth daughter of WOE, Test, she was born as a queen, she was a person of bitterness. Test went to the village, she was never noticed as she walked among the persons. In her heart she was their queen. She spoke only royal language of her own invention, no person could understand the orders she gave.

Test walked among the persons of the island, she spoke to each man. She made a demand, she made her first demand.

"Give me a daughter" she told each man of the island.

The men each laughed, the men each shook his head, the men each shrugged, the men each made the gesture of curling the hands at the chest. The men each closed his eyes and waited for this demand to pass away from him.

A man named Utu or "Incapable" was named that way by WOE. Now Test said to Utu: Change my face, change my eyes, you are my beloved. Create me again, give me a new name of your choosing. I will be yours. I have no companion. Do not make me to be alone.

Test made this demand.

Utu said: When I have to build a place for me to live, I laugh. I know I can not. When I have to create copper from stone, when I have to create glass from sand, I laugh. I know I can not. When I have to fell a tree and turn it to a boat, I laugh. I know I can not.

Now I must remove your garment. Now I must lay you down in the darkness. Now I must pour semen into you. Now I must bring your

baby out of you. Now I must feed you and your
child.

I am Utu. I have never seen myself do
these things. There is no one to explain these
things. I can not do these things, they make me
laugh. I will try, for a game. We can laugh as I
try. It will be funny, but it will not be done properly. But if you are serious, but if you are request-
ing, but if you are demanding, then you must go
to another man and request, you must go to
another man and demand.

That is what Utu said.

Test was queen of all the three worlds. A
queen does not accept refusal. She said: I was
wrong to make requests. They shall come to me.
That is what Test said. So that she returned home
immediately.

She told her sisters: By walking in the
village for seven hours, I have used up seven
selves. I have used up seven lives I can not live
again. I will not live another life, they do not
deserve it. That is what she said. And she sat on
the ground in the hut and died willfully.

When dead, when alone, when alone, when not with her sisters, when not with WOE, when dead, then Test was calm, then she was in love with any thing with a name. She could tell the soul of all persons and animals, also she could read the inner names of gods, she could read textures of any plant or stone.

More than any other person, Test had a face that saw things, she did not hate things, she loved things.

She gave love to every thing, she whispered the name of every thing, then she wanted her name whispered back. She wanted to hear her name whispered to her. Her name was never whispered to her.

She gave love, she whispered and sang, but her name was never whispered to her. She gave love, but her mouth became bitter.

She made small clay models of persons and things, and she loved these clay models. To the clay beings she was a generous queen, and they whispered her name to her, because she made them whisper her name.

Then her face moved freely and smiled, surprising words came from her, prayers and jokes and songs. She also sang to WOE, when WOE slept. She sang songs of warning. When WOE awoke, then Test slept.

At night, WOE dreamed she created the whole world.

In the day, WOE believed she created the whole world.

Island, no one knows you are an island. Island, the islanders believe you are the whole world. Island, your creator WOE believes she created the sun, the stars, the night, the day, the seas. Island, your creator WOE doesn't know about the lands beyond the island.

WOE has seen men in ships. But she has let herself forget. WOE has heard men in ships call to her. But she has let herself forget.

WOE believes her seven daughters are the chief gods of the world. As badly as her seven daughters behave, WOE thinks they are the fates of the world. As foolishly as her seven daughters speak, WOE thinks they are the greatest creation of all creation.

The seven, they are seven sisters, they are seven daughters. Each of them speaks with a differing voice. Each of their seven voices has seven musical tones. Each musical tone has seven textures. No daughter sounds like any other daughter. Yet all of them went to the village, all spoke, all could not be heard. They were all not heard in the similar way.

Hit, the seventh sister, the last daughter, the last born daughter, Hit kissed the faces of her sisters, she went to the village. Hit spoke to one person, she told her story to one person. She waited, she told her story and waited. She waited, starved, then she died. She was not fed, so that she died.

Hit was not fed. She saw a boy of the village, she spoke to him. He could not understand her. She spoke to him of her death. She spoke to him of her sisters' deaths. She spoke to him alone, she spoke into his ear. He did not understand. Then she could not speak further.

She stopped. She would not talk to boy. She stopped talking.

Once he came back to her and took off his clothing, but she would not reach out to him, so that he went away.

She forgot words when she saw him. She became not her own self.

She saw him. She forgot her name. She thought his name. His name was shallow, it did not reach back any place. The word of his name was shallow, it did not reach the second world or the third world.

She knew nothing about him, completely. All stopped in him. She became a picture, because he was a picture. A picture of a person is a face turned into a name.

A picture of a boy can not love you. Even though it (picture) looks full of love, it is full of an empty name.

She could not speak. She wanted to go into the picture, where nothing was. She wanted to stop being Hit entirely.

When alone, she prayed, she was strong,

86

her words were strong. Gods loved her words. She did not ever say her own name. If her sisters said "Hit" to her, she turned aside. She was beautiful like a thousand birds and she said: I know I am nothing.

Who can attain to be such a picture as she wished to be? By what shadow can such picture be seen?

Hit waited, she was ignored, she died. She was not fed, not even by one person. She emitted radiance, she was ignored. She spoke with a serious brow, she was not heard.

She said: If I knew how to tell a story, he would love me, he would feed me.

When she dreamed she forgot herself, she saw the boy, he danced with a stone tied to his legs, he had many grasping arms, he was a silly and joking artisan, he was a sour and earnest priest, he was a singing-bowl of flattery, he was charming like a floating feather.

She desired him, she desired his flattery. She desired his charm, she desired his empty charm. She desired his dance, she desired his

crippled dance. She desired his picture, she desired his false picture, she desired his flat picture,
she desired his picture. She stopped and she
waited, she was not fed. She died.

So that WOE came and took her daughter
home.

Why could not the daughters of WOE tell
a story? It is because stories were not in the world.
Praise WOE, no stories yet arrived in the world.
The life of a daughter, it was a hymn. The death
of a daughter, it was a hymn. The beauty of the
orchard, it was a hymn. The lightning-storm, the
brush-fire, these were hymns.

The story was not invented because the
cage was not invented. The cage was not invented
because the dungeon was not invented. The
dungeon was not invented because the castle was
not invented. The castle was not invented because
the soldier was not invented.

The soldier was not yet born, because the
elaborate structure was not yet invented. If a man
throws a stone at another man, the other man
becomes angry, shouts, he picks up a stone, he
strikes the first man. They both shout, they are

angry. They harm each other, they kill each other. It is over. That is not a story, it is not a book of pages. It is a hymn.

The stone is a god, STONE, the stone speaks its name when it strikes, the name is like dirt in the mouth of the man who throws the stone, the name is like embers in the mouth of the man who is struck. STONE sings the hymn. The men are changeable like water, STONE and the name "stone" are permanent. So that the stone will sing the hymn.

WOE first spoke the name of the stone. Praise WOE. The lake is stone, the stone fills with sweet water. Praise WOE. The seven daughters are ignored and die, they are harvested by WOE and they stay near her. All seven daughters are finished attempting to live, all are finished dying.

WOE spoke the name of every thing. She spoke the names of her seven daughters.

When she said "Opa," Opa was born and was already dead.

When she said "stone," the stone was

already thrown, the stone already killed the angry man.

When she said "honey" all persons already tasted honey, all persons knew honey on their tongues.

The word "honey." Do you understand? HONEY is with you, if you call. But also the date palm comes near you, also sweet water from the river, also a yellow sunrise comes to you. You need few words to bring the world to yourself.

Consider: you do not need the whole world. You need few parts of the world, with few parts of the world you have a place of opulence, you have syrup and wine and silk heaped up into piles, you have flesh, you have light.

Then why do you need a story? What is the utility of a story?

Honey on your tongue is the hymn of the word. No power can remove honey from "honey," no power can take HONEY from your tongue. Only forgetfulness does that. Forgetfulness is similarly sweet.

A story is to trap a word, maybe "honey," and enact other words against it. You can *eliminate honey* by telling a story against it. You can *eliminate honey* by telling a story of the war between honey and the kingdom of flowers. Such a war, which has never happened, will happen in the story. So that honey is made to fight, honey is cruelly tortured, honey is turned to dust and dark air, honey is turned to bitterness. This is the excitement of a story.

WOE never spoke "story," she never told a story, she never created STORY.

STORY came itself, in the moment of WOE's uncertainty.

Her seven daughters were dead, this was in the hymn, this was known from the beginning.

WOE sang their names, Opa, Twick, Glasp, Icic, Dif, Test, Hit. WOE sang their names. After the last name, WOE paused. She was trying to sing one name further. The name would not sing out of itself. NAME came to WOE and told her to sing freely. SONG pushed WOE out of the hut and told her to sing to the sky.

There was a missing name. There was an eighth daughter. There was a fate for the eighth daughter. There was a future incident that was not known. There was an arrival that had not arrived.

SONG battered WOE with noise, WOE stumbled into the chaff pile. WOE hid her mouth, she hid her throat, she hid her mouth from the sky. She prevented the naming of the unnamed.

WOE knew the name of the eighth daughter. She knew the end of the world, she knew the end, she saw the world's end. She saw her eighth daughter, she saw what that girl would do. She saw the deterioration. She saw the degeneration. She saw the aging. She saw the weakness.

She saw, WOE saw the birds die out of the air. She saw, WOE saw the birds she named die. She saw the birds she created die. She heard the bird songs she composed die.

WOE who named the hills, supreme over the lands, weaver of vegetation, winder of fish guts, womb of words, good-hearted creator of the horizon, what have you done? Maker of the three worlds, daughter of the former world, what have you done? The storm is yours, the lightning is yours, the wind is yours—why have you created a power greater than yourself?

Do not speak, WOE. Do not sing, we will sing for you, you must never sing again. Do not name the final name. What have you done, what have you done?

The untold, the unuttered, the silent, this was a story. The conflict, the collapse, this was a story. There was a story. WOE held her forearms over her mouth. But all creation knew there was a story now. The story would be told, to the last word.

THE ARRIVAL OF THE BOATS…THE ARRIVAL OF THE SPY: THE CAPTURE OF WORDS: DESTRUCTION OF THE CRE-ATION: MURDER OF WHITE SAILORS: A TOOTH CAN DIG OUT A RIVERBED: POI-SON COMES FROM THE EYES: HURLING-AWAY OF THE CORPSE: AN INJURY TO THE VOICE: CHANGE OF LANGUAGES: MEN BECOME FORMER MEN: NO FAITH IN GODS: SILENCE WILL OVERWHELM SOUND: THE DEATH OF THE MIST-TREE.

At that time there were fifty, there were fifty upon the beach, there were fifty who celebrated, there were fifty who watched the new sea-flower. Four large floating things in the sea, this was a new sea-flower. We watched from the beach, nature was creating anew, WOE was creating, we sent our hearts out to wrap around the new beauty, we sent our eyes out to praise the new beauty. We raised songs, we raised dances.

The ocean threw up four complex flowers, as the hair on the head of your beloved is complex, as cane juice leaves patterns on rock, the flowers were covered in vines and giant petals, they moved with the sea, they moved. We were overjoyed as when a hailstorm comes.

We then saw some men walking on the giant things.

We remained still. We did not speak any name.

When you heat the oil and wax together to make a mask, you heat it so it bubbles. You add the coloring juice. You hold the hot jar in one hand and berries squeezing in the second hand, this is a moment. This could be a moment. There could be a moment, when you slip and the hot stuff splashes down the front of you, your whole body is changed for the rest of time.

That would be a moment, the same as dropping a fish bait on the ground. You can pick up the fish bait again, you can not pick up your flesh again.

We still danced, but it was like falling down a hill. WOE was there with us, we looked to her eyes. The eyes of a creator know how to feel. We looked to see how to feel.

In the eyes of WOE, all our great boats became small. In the eyes of WOE, our world became one island, our entire world became an island. In the eyes of WOE, the things we all knew, we did not know. In the eyes of WOE, the strongest of us were weak persons, the tallest of us were short persons, the youngest of us were old persons.

The eyes of WOE saw greatness shine over the seas, it was not our greatness. The eyes of WOE saw light shine broadly over the sky, it was not our light.

WOE thought she created the world. She
did not create these giant boats. She did not know
the name for these boats. She did not know if they
were paintings of boats. They were too large. She
had not spoken of them. But WOE spoke of
"death," perhaps DEATH looked like this.

WOE did not create the world. WOE was
creator of an island in the world sea.

WOE did not know the size of the world.
WOE was the creator of a tiny island.

Any giant can float up to a tiny island and
take it.

On one of the giant boats, a thing happened. Out of the giant boat came a small boat.

We returned to our huts and waited for
death.

Our lives were at end, because a story
began, a story is taking place for the first time. A
story will always destroy everything.

This story would be told until we were killed by it, and a new world will begin. We became the creatures of the old world. We were an old story, we were a previous story.

Every thing looked the same. But it was a tiny island now. It was a story now. It was the past now.

Coming out of the small boat, walking among us, was a lightskinned person called Pigafetta. He put his hand to his chest and said the word "Pigafetta." This name never existed. He was a man who named himself. He was a man who created himself.

Terrified we waited to die.

WOE was lost to us. WOE was not in our reach. We spoke "Woe" and WOE did not appear with us. Because destruction arrived, then creation would depart.

We stood hidden, each apart from each. The women cried "I am the woman for whom bitterness has come." The men cried "I am the man for whom bitterness has come."

degenerescence

The women said "The swamp will take my body." The men said "The swamp will take my possessions."

The women said "The violent storm will take my peace and wisdom and leave me as a bleached skeleton." The men said "The violent storm will take my fame and my deeds, and leave me as a bleached skeleton."

The persons lamented for themselves alone. They lamented for their parents. They lamented for their children. They lamented for their sisters, brothers, husbands, wives.

They called on the word "Pigafetta." They called on the man Pigafetta. They requested PIGAFETTA to not decree the utter destruction of their village. Let not the persons perish. Let not the houses be burnt. Let not the gods be taken. Let not the gods be destroyed. Let not the words in our mouths be erased.

WOE, appease him. WOE, creator, appease him. Save us and appease him.

The persons of the village saw their severed heads upon the ground. They saw their

98

headless bodies uncovered. They saw the envelope of their flesh opened, and all the words removed. They saw their bodies without words.

Four giant boats watched while Pigafetta walked among our huts. Upon each hut Pigafetta set his eyes. Into each hut Pigafetta entered.

Each man, each woman was touched on the forehead by the hand of Pigafetta. Pigafetta who was the spy, Pigafetta who was the thief of words.

Pigafetta spoke nonsense to each of us, he spoke to unfamiliar gods. He made sounds that do not exist, and some of us tried to make those sounds. The true gods did not object, the true gods did not destroy us. Pigafetta listened, Pigafetta who was the spy, the thief of words, who holds paper and pen, Pigafetta who makes words mortal.

Pigafetta touched each person on the lips of the mouth, with his finger. He brought every person outside, and he pointed to each object in the world. We called the name of each god, we called the god of each object. We ourselves told him the names of all the words of all the gods of all things! He captured all the names onto his paper. He took all the names, then folded his papers, the papers went into his clothing so that they were a part of him.

WOE, he then could speak. By signs of our words, he spoke. Our words came from his mouth.

He said: Who is the "story teller" here.

We did not understand that.

He said: Who makes all the "stories."

We did not know that word.

He said: Who created the world. Pigafetta said: Who created the world.

WOE, we told him your name.

WOE, your name is the air in our mouths. Your name is the threshold to our chests. Your name is strong as an ash tree beside the river. We told Pigafetta your name, we gave your name to him!

Your name is the momentum of heaven below our feet. The movements under our feet, the souls under our feet. Your name is the hymn without end, the word without a destroying word, the telling of nothing but what is. Your name is the purifying hand. We told Pigafetta your name. We gave your name to him!

WOE, your name is our death, your name is the flow of unmoving life, it is the seal that preserves the meaning of birds, it is the clamor in all words. Your name is the cessation of the heartbeat, it is the silence in the heartbeat. We told Pigafetta your name, we gave your name to him!

O error, retreat and forgive us, error, return to your home in the sky. Error that destroys the future, return. This is the error that turned the world to an island. This error, this error began to tell a "story." In this error we created age, we created degeneracy. In this error we created words that have no feeling in the mouth. We created stupidity, we created ambition and drama. In this error we created the generality. We told the name of WOE, we gave away the name.

When Magellan comes, when he...

the mighty king who...

when I, WOE, shrink to a single point and vanish, when I shrink, when he honors us and comes, when he...

when he...

when he comes to us and brings the outer world, when he creates the outer world, when he unsettles the inner world, when he...

when...

when he unsettles...

He is the Obstacle, all praise him. He shrinks the sky to a single point, praise him.

Magellan, he is everywhere, we applaud him, we change our voices, we change our feelings. When he comes from the boats, he destroys songs, he destroys songs, we applaud him.

He utters a challenge against WOE, he knows the name of WOE, he mocks at WOE, he withers the vines, he withers the trees. He is the Builder, he is the path-layer.

WOE says: I did not know this thing existed.

WOE says: I have been wrong. I have been wrong. I have told lies. I have not created the world. This is not the world. This, here, this, this is not the world, this is not the world.

WOE will not change her voice, she will cease to speak. WOE will stop speaking and stop singing, so that the words of Magellan will prevail, the words we do not know will prevail, the words we will never understand will prevail.

Magellan teaches fate. He tells us our fate. He walks with black darkness. We are full of black darkness. We are of the mud. Magellan is the god of the mud.

The sky is mud, it is made of mud. The sun is mud, to which someone has fastened a golden disc. Remove the disc to see the truth, the sun is of mud, the sun is mud.

The past is mud, it is of mud, also the

future is not even mud, the future is not going to exist. Magellan holds the future, he will keep it. Whoever believes we are full of light, that person is of the mud.

Magellan tells the stories. He tells the story of Europa. The story continues forever, the story is mockery, it is withering mockery. The story does not believe its words, its words are not from the three worlds, its words have no ground, its words have no air.

WOE, who escaped the mockery of the former world, WOE in her white garment, WOE, WOE in her black garment, WOE who created the present world, WOE who created a world for herself to live in in her white garment, a world of peace, to live in in her black garment, a world of peace, WOE has to see all her own words topple into a story full of withering, a story full of mouth laughter, a mocking story.

WOE walks the entire world she created, to find a place to be. The world is only an island, the world is small. She can not bury herself under the mountain. She can not hide under the sea. She can not hide in the top of the sky. She has walked around the entire earth, it is a small island. She is on the fish-netting beach where she began.

All persons change their minds. WOE's
seven daughters change their minds. Glasp buries
her clothing, she creates a Magellanic clothing.
The daughters stamp around the cedar trees, the
daughters play at being Portugal persons or
Europa persons. They wear the hats Glasp makes
for them.

We assuaged Magellan, we gifted him
with pigs, four boats of cloves, four boats of fig,
six vessels of betel, many painted boxes and jars,
feathers of our best birds, also two of the birds
themselves. Also we gave him the son and daughter of a middle wife of our calmest man and three
small deer.

We gave these gifts in humiliation, they
were small dark gifts, they were small stunted
gifts, they were improper gifts of the nature of
garbage. They were subject to rot and deterioration.

Magellan gifted us in return as follows:
green silk, red cloth, mirrors, scissors, knives,
combs, and two gilt glasses. He caused brass
drums to be played, which astonished us all with

its spirited noise. The soldiers also played a kind of viol, and a wooden horn called serpent.

We accepted these gifts in humiliation. We wanted to boast of our island, but it was an island. We wanted to boast of our island, but our boasting was in the wrong language. We are not now real. We never were real. We are not the world.

WOE, whose size expands and contracts. WOE, whose voice is alone, whose voice is the size of the entire world or island. WOE, whose creation is the entire earth or island. WOE, who is I, when she is small. WOE, who is all persons, when she is large, WOE, we retreat from you.

WOE without faith is the size of a single point. WOE without faith is without voice. WOE without faith is without words. WOE, we retreat from you, we abandon you. When you abandon us, when you retreat from us, then we abandon you, we retreat from you.

The seven daughters of WOE, they had no voices to speak, they had no mother, they were not real, they were unmeaning, they wept, they wept without words. They wept without even the meaning of weeping, they wept without the god for "weeping," the word for "sorrow" was gone, SORROW was gone. The daughters of WOE could not weep fully.

The moon rises, the moon brings forth water, the moon carries light, it carries kindness, it rounds all words. On this night we all stared upon the disc of the moon. The temple of the moon, it was not our temple. The moon was a new world in the sky, the moon was apart, the moon was a place we could see clearly, we could sing to it, we could speak to it, we could sing our worthless songs and speak our worthless tongue. The moon was a place we could see but never visit. We were never there. Our boats are too small to go there. We wept, until we wished for a king who would tell us a lie, a king who would tell us: I will go there in a boat.

We wanted a king. We did not know the seven daughters, we did not know the seven sisters. They sing hymns to us, they are womanly, their voices can make the heart fly, their hymns can make water sing, their arms are pleasing, they stand and sit sweetly. They are not beloved, they look among us for one who will hear their voices. They are too tall, they are too short, they are too

much enfolded in hymn, they are too much
enfolded in words, they are too much enfolded in
silence. They look among us, they see no beloved.
We did not see them, we wanted a king to love.
From a king we would accept hymns, from a king
we would see beauty, from a king we would hear
beauty. We would see the beauty of a king, we
would hear the beautiful voice of a king. Where is
our king?

In the past, in the distant past, kings lived
on this island. They were kings of the entire
world. They were chosen king because they were
the most wise or most gentle.

Now, in the moon light, we chose a king.
He was the most strong. He had strong thighs, he
had strong shoulders. He spoke loudly, he covered
the land with his walking. We raised him up to
king, we created him king. We named him with
"king" so that KING came to him, moon blessed
him, WOE nodded her head silently to him. We
praised our strong king and loved him.

The seven daughters, the seven sisters,
they gave out their hymns, they died and returned
to their mother. They asked WOE, their mother,
to give birth an eighth time, to birth out an eighth

daughter, who would change the mind of the world, who would be perfect, who would be beloved, who would be the true king, who would be the true ruler.

WOE wept without speaking. She gave her daughters a task to do with their hands, so they would not ask for anything more. WOE burnt sand with fire, she blew into bamboo, she made glass. She made the blowing-out of glass. She showed her daughters the moon, she showed them glass, then she left them. WOE retreated and shrank to a single point with no voice, so that her daughters, weeping, made glass jars that looked like moons.

Each made a different jar of differing colors.

These jars they sat in the sand in the moon, in the light of the moon, glass jars sat in the light of the moon.

None of these jars could store food, none of these jars could hold water, none of these jars could keep insects, none of these jars could keep bait for fish. None of these jars could ferment matta, these jars were useless. They shone in the moon in colors, they shone in the sun in the colors plum, rose, violet, hazel, jade, emerald, amber. They did nothing else.

The daughters of WOE have eyes. Their eyes are beautiful and useless. They can look upon glass jars. Their voices are beautiful and useless. Their bodies are beautiful and useless.

The daughters of WOE have tried and failed. They have told their songs and failed. They have loved and failed. They have walked among persons and remained lonely.

The daughters WOE created, all are dead. WOE's daughters, all are dead. They make glass jars now, they make objects no person could wish to own.

You have died. Do not accuse. Do not blame the Europas for your failing. Do not blame Magellan for your being small. Do not blame Pigafetta for your being mute.

When WOE falls asleep, she sees the moon. She does not own the moon.

When WOE awakens, she sees the sun,

she sees the world. Her eyes are like light. When WOE first used her eyes, she created light. When WOE awakens, she creates light. She does not fear.

I am the milk of the sun. I am all beauty in the land. My hand is all the destroying weather, my hand sinks the boats of the Europas. My anus is the field that grows food, my anus starves the Europas. My foot is the mountain, my foot falls upon the Europas.

I am the battle, I am the entire war, I am the end of the world. I will end the Europas, I will end the entire world. I am the flood, I am the fire.

WOE has been offended by the man Magellan, WOE has been offended. The world belongs to her, she will return the world to herself.

WOE shines down from the sky with her light. She has a black stone dagger in her belt.

No power can change her. But she is changed.

If she must become a ball of flame, if she

must destroy, then she is forced to become a ball of flame. It is not her wish. She is forced to destroy, it is not her wish.

WOE who can do any thing, can not prevent this.

She plans that she will kill Magellan. That is the story. She knows the outcome, it has not happened yet.

When WOE created the world, she did not know the outcome. The names came to her mouth, the names created themselves, they surprised her. The world she created, she looked on it as a child looks.

A child does not kill, because a child does not change the world. But if WOE will kill Magellan, if WOE removes Magellan's name from his body, if WOE removes MAGELLAN from out of Magellan, so that he is uncreated, then all persons will be cursed, all persons will live within stories, all persons will tell themselves stories all through the day, all persons will never look on the world as a child does.

WOE knows this is the outcome, she can

not prevent this.

If WOE will kill Magellan, the story will never cease, other Europas will arrive, her islanders will be changed, her islanders will be uncreated, her islanders will believe they are inferior. They will lose their anger, they will lose their speed, they will lose their gracefulness, they will lose their joy, until one dried reed will be more great than this island. One dried reed will be more able to fill the chest and fill the throat and fill the eyes with floods of awe, mists of awe, one dried reed will be more than all her daughters, one dried reed will be more than all her islanders. The dried reed will float away and there will be nothing. WOE knows the outcome, she can not prevent it.

The king said: WOE, your creation is full of loveliness. You have a dagger, but the dagger is not yours. The dagger is not yours, I am strong, I am the king. I will take the dagger for you, I will kill Magellan for you.

The king, even he, the king made a story. He said I will kill Magellan for you.

WOE said: My brother, when you have

killed Magellan for me, what will happen next?

The king said: Beloved—after I kill Magellan, the other islanders will gouge him with rocks and spears.

WOE said: My brother, after they have gouged him, what will happen next?

The king said: Beloved—after they gouge him, Magellan will put a curse on our world.

WOE said: My brother, once he has put his curse, what will happen next?

The king said: Beloved—I will try to overcome the curse for you! I will try to overcome the curse!

WOE said: My brother, after you have tried, what will happen next?

The king said: Beloved—I will fail to overcome the curse, and the mist-tree will die. The source of our fresh water, the mist-tree, will die.

WOE said: My brother, after the tree dies,

what will happen next?

The king said: Beloved—then the tree will dry, it will be without leaves at the next dawn. No cloud will form around it. No water will come out from it. No birds will be born there.

WOE said: My brother, with the tree dry, what will happen next?

The king said: Beloved—I will bring you coconuts to drink from! I will bring you fruit and coconuts!

WOE said: My brother, what will happen next?

The king said: Beloved—you will drink fruit and coconuts, but you will always be thirsty. A man will climb a rock to drink the blue sky. Children will drink from drawings of the word "water" on the stone walls. All will be thirsty.

WOE said: My brother, if all are thirsty, what will happen next?

The king said: Beloved. Beloved, I do not know. Will we all die? Beloved, you know the outcome, Beloved, what will happen next?

WOE said: Any story, once begun, is already told, down to the very last name.

WOE gave to the king her pointed dagger, her black stone dagger.

WOE, she saw a river, though there was no river in the island.

The powerful king lifted a log, the king laid a log across the river. WOE saw this. Then the king put his arms around Magellan. The king walked with Magellan, they crossed the river on the log of a tree.

As they walked, the corpse of Magellan floated below them on the waters, the corpse of Magellan's body floated past them and floated away. Magellan saw his corpse, and was afraid.

Magellan. Afraid of Magellan the fish swim away. Magellan, afraid of him the rain falls upward. Magellan who frightens even the stones so that they turn dark. Magellan saw his corpse, he was afraid. Magellan was afraid.

WOE saw this. WOE heard Magellan
curse the island, curse the people, curse all island
people, curse all lands outside his own island of
Europa, curse all towns and settlements except the
one where he was born, curse all mothers except
his mother, curse all houses except his house,
curse all persons who are not himself. Magellan,
who did not want to die, said I will die, but not in
this place, not in such a place, not in such a garbage place.

He of the jewels across his neck muscles,
he of the golden skin, he of the metallic shine, he
of the curled hair, he of the soft beard, he of the
tall stature, he who brought great boats across
heaven, he says that I am garbage, he says that we
are garbage, he says that our world is garbage.
This is what he says while he dies.

His body floats away. His spirit turns to
us and speaks the word for garbage, it speaks our
own word for garbage, it speaks "speka," and we
feel the presence of the word.

WOE would wish to sing. She does not
sing. In a song is no past, in a song all feelings are
one feeling, in a song all feelings are at once. In a
song is no past, but in this island is a past. The

past is before Magellan threw his curse, the past is where we wish to return. WOE who can do all things, can not return to the past. She would like to sing, she would wish to be able to sing.

At night we hear the sea and we hear Magellan's voice saying sea, sea, his voice speaking our word. Ourselves speak the word, we speak it the way he spoke it, we forget how we used to say.

We forget, because his soldier Pigafetta, the man who wrote all things down, he asked us the names of things by pointing. He pointed, then he did not speak the name. It was impossible for us to be silent, we were forced to speak the name.

Now we speak "sea" and "rock" as Magellan spoke it, as Pigafetta spoke it. SEA and ROCK are not pleased to be sung this way. They escape in part, they escape, they leak away.

Magellan came and was killed, then we told that story. That was our first story. We harmed the words then. We spoke: *Ships came on the sea* so that we ruined the sea and many foods within it. *The arrows flew*, that ruined the air. *We buried the sailors* spoiled the whole of the ground.

The mist-tree, it died as WOE foretold it to. It was dead so that it made us no more water in the morning, and so that no birds were born there. We heard WOE calling out a song: Ploughing with the voice, ploughing with the voice, for whom am I ploughing? May the water be sweet, may the water be jewels for our throats. WOE sang that.

She was ploughing to make the river. She sang to tell us of the death of Magellan.

WOE explained: Magellan lived by the word, he lived upon words. So that WOE sang, so that she reversed words, she sang:

When you make the city a horse, when you make the bird into tears, when you put the inside of the spindle into the sky, when you set your foot into questioning, when you lie down upon strength,

so that river-mounds are not river-mounds, so that snake-venom will not be snake-venom, so the temple is interpreted as a topaz, so that a boy is not a boy, so that a youth is wise, so that an old man gives birth, and you replace the sky with a sky, you replace your feet with your feet, you replace the matta you drink with the matta you drink, you replace your life with your life. Then you can die, and join yourself, and die, and join yourself.

That is the song WOE sang. Magellan's body flowed past Magellan at that time.

The world needed water, the persons needed to drink, the animals needed to drink. The world or island was occupied in its mind with water, all persons were thinking of the same water at the same time, all were worried about one thing, there was stoppage, life was not good to live. WOE took the body of Magellan, stabbed by the king, the body of the great traveler and boat-wielder Magellan, she took the body and pulled out the front tooth. With this tooth she carved the River Swastika in three days' time.

And the king pulled out the other front tooth, and he carved the Lesser River Swastika to placate and purify the waters of the first river, in case this first river should be a terrible mistake.

Then the body of Magellan: WOE and king put the body of Magellan at the place where

the two rivers begin, so that the water came from
his eyes. The Greater Swastika came from his
right eye, and the Lesser Swastika came from his
left eye.

Persons heard the sound of flowing water,
water flowed, it continued, it flowed unceasingly,
the water flowed. Where the water from the mist-
tree appeared once per day, like a flowering of
water, now was constantly a continuing of water
without stop. Nothing is without stop but now
water is without stop, fearsome. The water spoke
words that were senseless or new. The village
heard the water talk in constant water words.
Now words would not stop.

Six villagers came to speak to WOE and
ask her the meaning of the words of the river. She
listened, first she listened, then she spoke, saying:
I hear one word. I hear one song with two notes. I
hear a song of one word, with two notes. Nothing
changes, it is peaceful, it is a song, it is a hymn.

The villagers cried: We hear a thousand
words! We hear a thousand senseless words! The
villagers felt more alone, the villagers felt they
were not understood by WOE, their fears were
not known to WOE.

We will all be chaff, they cried, we will all enter stories and be forgotten at the close of the story.

We will all become dust, the words of our names will be emptied out, the river will drown our voices. We will be water, we will be dust, we will be nonsense sound, we will be indistinguishable from air, we will be indistinguishable from all other named things. All names will be one name that will not cease to be spoken. There must be silence, we beg for silence. WOE, who created this disaster, WOE, creator of noise, we pray for silence.

WOE, who can do all things, could not create silence out of noise.

Magellan, his dead self, kept his name and ran the rivers. In our language "Magellan" is the name for the greater world. "Magellan" is the name for the obstacle. "Magellan" contains the ordinary words, the words you use to ask for food, the words you use to thank the cook, the words you use with your father-in-law, the polite words, the story words, the ordinary words. "Magellan" means one thing follows another. "Magellan" means water runs downhill. There is no singing his name. There is no singing the name of Magellan.

Now WOE must listen to every villager, Every villager speaks, every villager speaks at the same time. They are each telling stories. They tell of the death of Magellan, they tell this, they tell this story one hundred different ways. They tell the creation of the world. They tell the destruction of the island. These stories are long, they contain journeys, arguments, discoveries, battles, kings, princes, gods, hidden caves, murders, revenge, love, concealment, misunderstanding, inner thoughts, reasons, lies, flying blankets, swords, magic, victories, these stories are full of the future, these stories fill the future, the future becomes full, the future becomes complete, the future becomes completed.

WOE sleeps, she sees a dream. In her dream, WOE hears every word of every village story, and she carries them (words) to the wall, she places them against the sky above the wall, and she shrinks the sky to a single point, and she tells all these stories by singing a single note. WOE who created every word makes every word return to her mouth. She hums.

Upon waking from her dream, WOE found the world infested with stories. WOE became cautious. WOE became unwilling to speak aloud. May WOE not change. That WOE can create worlds, may she not change. That WOE can invent new words, may she not change. That WOE weeps for her daughters, may she not change. That WOE is of childbearing age and can produce an eighth daughter, may she not change. That WOE speaks her own words, that WOE speaks no Europa words, tells no stories, sings in rituals, shrinks the sky, has the thoughts of WOE, has the dreams of WOE, may she not change.

WOE threw down her clay flute, WOE changed. She threw down her flute. WOE, whose hair flows over the sea, she threw down her flute.

The island persons, created-by-WOE persons, they are like grain, they have flowed into a new vessel. The persons have composed one hundred stories about the creation. They have composed one hundred stories about Magellan. They have composed one hundred stories about each one of the persons of the village.

Created-by-me persons have done this foreign thing. I am WOE. I am as strong as this island world. I am as strong as this encircled world. I am as strong as this flooded, infiltrated world. I existed prior to water, but I was silent then. I existed prior to the foreigners, but I was ignorant then. I made no distinction between honey, rats, swords or birds, when I first spoke those names. If rats are not as beautiful as honey, if rats are not as aware as birds, if rats are to be condemned even above swords, then I am wrong, my words are wrong, my eyes are wrong, my island is wrong. If I must protect myself from creation, if I must hide from the words of others, if stories are normal, if I am not normal, then the cave of the heart of all creatures is empty.

I protected seven babies, and saw them die. But I will not protect myself.

I gave my island to a foreigner, then I killed him. But I will not flee, I will not hide.

What is within me is also every place. What is every place is within me. I must have invented stories, I must have invented fate, I must have invented tedium, I must have invented drinking alcohol, I must have invented lies, I must have invented pain. I will not insult the names of these things, I will not insult the forms of the gods, I will not insult the gods of these names. I will stop speaking, rather than use their names in story telling, I will stop speaking and remain silent rather than trap the gods in a story. I will become mute rather than ruin the objects of the world by using them to decorate stories.

I am the size of a thumb, my island is the size of a jar, my silence will make no difference among these thousand speaking voices. But I will not pretend to be happy, I will not put my heart into the furnace and talk it away.

I am the size of a drop of water, I travel down the mountain, I split into streams. The man who thinks that is a story, he gets lost in many streams.

A drop of water is enough. The man who sees it, he is satisfied.

I hear a word as I hear my own breath. I hear a hymn as I hear my heart beat. I hear a note on the flute as I hear the footsteps of my own people. I hear a story as I hear a shadow that falls over the light.

When I sleep, then I awaken and say this rhetoric:

THE MISERY OF WOE...A DAUGHTER SHE DID NOT HEAR: INCOMPLETE BABY: FEARFUL ISLANDERS: MURDER OF MAGELLAN: THE CURSE AND THE RIVER: SEVEN DAUGHTERS MOURN: SPANIARDS IN BRONZE: THE DESTRUCTION OF MUSIC: BRITON IGNORANCE: AN ARMY DEFEATS ITSELF: MURDER OF ALL FOREIGNERS: PLAGUE OF IMPOTENCE: WOE LEAVES THE ISLAND FOREVER: THE WRECK OF THE ISLAND: WEEPING OF MEN AND WOMEN. THE MISERY OF WOE.

Before this story began, there was no River Swastika flowing through the island, neither the Greater nor Lesser Swastika. The island was without a shape. There was no arrangement to the colors. There were no roots underground.

We had the mist-tree. Each morning, the sun struck the tree in the east, a cloud formed around the tree, the tree vanished in cloud. Tree, no-roots-tree, unseen tree. In daylight, all the leaves dropped, we went to collect them. They were pods full of sweet water.

At night, more leaves grew out. This happened all the year. All the year was the same and there was no border to a year, there was no border to the time.

In those days you passed your hand in front of your face and did not know your hand was there. Motions of your body had the form of rustling sounds. Speech was murmur all the day and night. Speech did not come from voices of persons. Speech was in the earth.

Birds of those times had long feathers. Birds were born with differing colors each morning, according to the color of cloud around the mist-tree.

After Magellan came, after Magellan disturbed the world, after Magellan offended the gods of words, after Magellan died upon a log bridge, after Magellan fed two rivers, then no birds were born in a colored mist.

Blue, orange and jade birds lost their names, their names lost the souls of names, the birds were lost. They were called birds, meaning "world birds." They could not change their name to "island birds."

WOE looked at the sea, WOE was the size of the point of a knife. The sea was much larger than the former sea. Before Magellan came, the sea was called "sea," meaning the water gird of the world. It could not change its name to Path toward the World, Distance from the World, Sea of Enemies, Sea of Darkness.

If the sea has no weight, if the sea has no depth, if the sea has no color, if the sea has no smell, if the sea has no taste, if the sea has no sand, if the sea is no good to work in or play in, then it loses the faith of its name. The word "sea" has nothing of SEA and the sea has nothing of SEA.

Every other name and thing on the island came into such a condition also. Each tree was without its god. The red fish was without its god. The spear point was without its god. Every thing you can name lost the faith of its name.

There is a fire lit: the fire has lost the faith of its name. Persons look into the fire, the fire fails to hold the eye. The fire fails to speak to the eye.

WOE, whose spoken speeches are permanent, whose words are bone, who is made of
words, who holds the souls of words: where is
your voice, where is your language, where is your
creation?

Now persons meet in a group every night,
around a false fire. The persons are thirsting for a
story.

One man tells a story to all. His story
makes every person listen. Every utterance makes
you laugh. His story creates a foolish woman,
every utterance makes you laugh at the foolish
woman, at her foolish husband, at the stupid dog
owned by them.

Every utterance of the story is made of a
false word, put together with a word that used to
be true.

The listeners have nothing they can see.
No thing is created here. The listeners look into
the fire, to try to see. The fire is dark, the fire is
not enough bright.

They hear the utterances, they hear the story. LAUGHING does not want to be laughed but LAUGHING laughs upon being forced to laugh.

The story teller, he shouts, he says he sees this woman, he sees her husband, also the dog. He shouts as if the woman is concentrated out of ten women, as if the husband is concentrated out of ten men, as if the dog is concentrated out of ten dogs.

What is wrong in this story, what is terrible in this story, what is missing from this story that must be added, what is within this story that must be removed?

Persons are laughing at a woman and a man and a dog. The woman is trapped, the man is trapped, the dog is trapped. They can do only the things that are funny. They can say only the things that are funny. The man and woman and dog, they will die without singing, they will die without dreaming, they will die without walking, they will die without sitting alone, they will die without thinking, they will die apart from every other soul, they will die and never live beneath the earth, they will never live after the story ends.

They are being told, they are being told by
STORY, they are trapped, they will die.

The story teller shouts, and the woman
and man and dog are bright, terrible, they flame
in the night, they hurt the eyes. There is nothing,
it is dark, it is not enough bright. His story is a
burial. His story cuts short the life of those who
hear it. His story is a sharp dagger, his story is a
baited trap.

WOE, when you made the world, there
was no falsehood. You held out a word, there was
the word in your hand.

WOE, you who created the world, you can
not explain. You can make a hymn, but you can
not make a story and explain.

Your muteness was the foundation of the
world. Your muteness, it is a crack in the world.
Your muteness will be the destruction of the
world. You are a failure. You are mute.

In the times before these times, the first
story was told. WOE, you are mute. So that
Magellan told the first story. He said "Tomorrow
I will bring gifts." We all heard him. He spoke

"gifts" and GIFT listened, GIFT sang for us all the night. Magellan spoke "gifts" even though no gifts were before us.

We saw the gifts. The words came from his mouth, the words were gifts, we saw gifts. We slept the night dreaming of unseen gifts. Our huts piled high with unseeable gifts. We gifted ourselves with GIFT, and GIFT gave us transparent gold, floating boxes, silver water moving through tubes in the sky, whirling statues whose faces changed every moment. We saw lambs made of pig, pigs made of fish, a song of blue stone that fit under the tongue and sang out. Magellan spoke our word for gifts, he changed our word for gifts.

Magellan, tomorrow he then brought gifts. They did not match. They did not match what we saw. We wept, we heard a story, we believed a story about the future, it diverted us, it was bright, it was false.

A false story does not happen, but it is true while it is told. WOE said this.

A true story would say:

The sun rose up, the sea waves waved.

The sun continued in rising. The sea waves continued the waving.

The sun, the waves. The sun, the waves.

WOE told that story to her daughters. She told another true story, saying: A true story would be every word that does now appear.

Cinnamon, banana, stone, eyes, fishnet, mouse.

This story can be believed. But it can not be listened to.

When her daughters left home to go to the village and speak, WOE told them this rhetoric:

Tell stories that can be listened to. Tell true stories that can be listened to. Create a true story that can be listened to. Speak each word with honor to the god, speak each word as you sing. You are the beautiful singers of the world, you are the beautiful singers of the known and unknown world, you are the beautiful singers of the three worlds. Speak stories with the same care as you sing.

WOE said all this, to each daughter, this is what she said. Every daughter heard her.

After her daughters died, they did not believe her words. They questioned her words.

They said:

If a word were a god, would I not worship this word? I am speaking just now. A speaking, a rhetoric, leaves no time to worship each word. I refuse to speak so slowly.

Nothing wrong happens if I ignore words. I will ignore words as I speak them.

If a word were a god, speaking would cause:

the ocean to boil,

the mountain to crumble,

the birds to explode in the sky,

the eyes of the fish to turn to fire,

the children to grow to a thousand miles in length,

the songs to turn to snow,

the speeches to turn to goat's milk,

the trees to turn to fountains of sugar,

the houses to fill with pink smoke,

the multitudes of humans to fall into the dust,

the multitudes of insects to raise into the sky.

That is how her daughters spoke to WOE.

WOE heard them. Then as they watched, WOE spoke one word.

It was a word they did not know.

And the ocean boiled, the mountain crumbled, the birds exploded in the sky, the eyes of the fish turned to fire, the children grew to a thousand miles in length, the songs turned to snow, the speeches turned to goat's milk, the trees turned to fountains of sugar, the houses filled with pink smoke, the multitudes of humans fell into the dust, the multitudes of insects raised into the sky.

Seven daughters saw these. They became persons who spoke with great care, terrible care.

They became those persons you see who do not speak.

It is too hard to speak. Only to ask for bread, this means the statement or prayer, "bread." To speak "bread" is to pray to these things:

"food" things	"grain" things
"dry" things	"plant" things
"soft" things	"growing" things
"brown" things	"flour" things
"light" things	"yeast" things
"smaller" things	"heated" things
"scent" things	"taste" things

Minutes of thought and attention will pass before "bread" can be fully spoken.

So that to speak such an utterance as:

"The girl with the copper skin has injured her hand by pulling on the fishnet, so that her blood is falling on the sand of the beach,"

this would take too much care, too much care. Such speaking is for a great saint to speak. Such speaking is beyond the height of the sky.

For us on this island, the story telling stopped within us, within us the voice of STORY feared to speak. Such sudden lack of stories was a new thing upon the earth. Now the listeners blinked their eyes. Now the listeners cleared their ears. Now the listeners stopped hearing a story, they stopped seeing vivid gods, they turned from listeners into persons. Instead of a story, they now had light, and food, smell of a hut, a face of a wife which is better than all descriptions, a bird call better than songs, an island better than stories.

Here is the explanation. When WOE first spoke, she spoke a poem, the creation of the world was a poem or song. WOE spoke a poem 100,000 slokas in length, scattering all objects throughout the world, also making the shapes of things. The way the sea leans on the land, that was formed of a sloka or verse. The tree in the ground is "tree" and "ground" but they were put together first in lines in the poem.

Sometimes the person who is story teller will say a sentence that makes the listener feel uncanny. Bright WOE raises her head, we are in the place of calm, we see a shining metal, we see the curving sky.

Such a speaker has by accident spoken some words of the old poem. Even to put two words of the old poem together as before, that will make the black earth of heaven open. If we can hear a few whole lines of poem as it was, we will live forever, we will fly, we will float.

Words are every place, we know them all. We do not manage to tell the ancient poem over. The more we talk, the more our words disorder themselves.

The words fly apart as soon as spoken. We are desolated. We are without divinity. We are without WOE, we are without love. The gods will not touch each to each. They will not hold hands and circle us here. They will not protect us here. They fly apart as soon as they are spoken.

WOE, speak for us. WOE, why do we speak?
WOE, speak for us.

Life is yet to be completed, no life is
completed, a life is not completed. Look at eating
a meal. You eat a meal of food, you are satisfied.
Your satisfaction is like peace, it is like fame, it is
like love, it is like the color white in the down of
the bird, it is the bleached sea shell, the pearl, it is
milk, the whole egg, a sand flower, spotless, it is
the moon or the white star, it is like laughter.

However, while you eat your meal: in your
hut is the rat in the corner, who sleeps, and the rat
turns in sleep, it dreams.

While you eat your meal, the bird of long
feathers waits on your roof to begin its search.

While you eat your meal in your hut,
while you are satisfied, a sunlight on the wall
moves and causes a ripple, it moves and makes a
new life without a name.

When the island is destroyed, destruction
will be one thing that will happen. Other things
will also happen. When I die, when I lose my
name, when the name WOE is detached, when

WOE in me returns to the second world, when I die, then also a fish will swim, also the sun will turn, also a wave will come, also a leaf will blow.

Instead of looking at my destruction, I will look at the leaf. To look at a leaf can be very boring after one minute. Then boredom returns to the place where leaves blow to. The desire to hit or rip the leaf returns to the place where leaves blow to. The leaf continues.

There are one million of leaves, also one million of red sunsets, also one million of clouds, also one million of stars, also one million of words and names and kinds of things. Each one is eating a meal. Each one is having seven daughters. Each one is blowing away with the breath of the speech of words.

I speak for WOE, I worship the first speaker, I praise WOE, I remain loyal to WOE. At the time when young persons do the most talk, at the time young persons do the most of joking and impure singing, that is when I am mute, I am mute like WOE, I become WOE.

The names of words are shouted as noise all over. The names of words, they hide from me.

At night, if nobody speaks to me, and I listen, then each name will come and speak itself.

I ask to sing. Let me sing the song of the song. I ask to sing WOE into existence. I ask to sing the creator of the world into existence.

WOE will help me, until the birth of her last daughter, her eighth daughter. Her last daughter will destroy, she will only destroy.

Destruction is the way to purify words.

The destruction of the earth will make the story to end.

Stories are gods fighting, they are words fighting. They are gods set to fighting, as the Dyaks set roosters to fight each other.

The battle is great. The gods create wonders. The battle is strong and persistent. It will never decay. The story will never decay. It will never stop on its own, it will never degenerate, it will never grow quiet. It will never cease to tell a story, until it is destroyed, until it ends in destruction, until it is killed, until the story is killed, until the world will end in quiet and quiet will begin.

Stories are for old persons to speak. Young persons will not listen to a story. Stories are not women's skin, stories are not matta, they do not dance. Young persons will not sit in a place to listen, they must laugh, they must dance.

Without young persons, no ewe would bring forth a lamb, no woman would bring forth a child, no thread would ever be tangled, no delight would ever be taken, bottles and jugs would never be thrown and broken for joy, the gods of joy would die while waiting. The wisdom of old persons will not keep JOY and DESTRUCTION alive.

Early times are for old persons to think of. Early times are not full of grain, they are not full of fish, they are not full of matta or love. Early times are not living, old times are not living.

Youths mumbled, also youths used grammar that was non-correct or new. So that the gods were harmed, the gods were hurt in their bodies. Fish were poisoned, the earth hardened, flowers turned to rock, rocks turned to hot steam. No person could sleep, no person could wake properly.

WOE did not care. She laughed.

WOE is drunk as she says the following statement: I will run my words along without listening. I am tired of being a slave. I am WOE, the creator. Let words pay respect to themselves. Let them respect me. I am a word, I am the name of WOE. I am a god, I am a word, I am a woman. Let words tremble to not offend me. Why should I be careful how I speak? We will end up sinking, with our pile of words.

The daughters of WOE abused all the names, all the names. They mumbled, also they shouted. They threw objects, they broke objects, they threw objects in the sea.

So the gods were harmed, they were hurt in their bodies. All youths shouted: Let us destroy the named objects of this island. Let the gods die so the earth will be what it is.

They spoke, sang, swore as they felt. They cursed the gods for fun, using the curse words to call each god a pig in turn. They made things rhyme that should not.

WOE sat with the youths and played their games, she sat with them and mocked the gods with joy. She said: My daughters are dead. What would be a faith in words? Like a faith in dirt.

How is this possible? WOE.

WOE, I long to understand you.

I long to stop hating you. WOE, I long to stop hating you with my heart.

I detail your faults every moment. It is my way of prayer. What are you, WOE? Why are you within me so that I can not forget you?

You are never old and never young. You are on every side of every dispute. You say every word in every language. I fault you and I am always right, and I am always wrong in faulting you.

What shall I say about you? Why do you let me speak to you? Why do you let me live?

If you would destroy me today, it would

be an easement.

I see you and you never stop speaking, and you are always silent. I call on you and you do not arrive, and you are always here.

You love, you are hurt. You hate, you are ignored. You dream, you wake yourself. You run, you move backwards. If you are a god you are the weakest and worst. If you are the creator, you are the weakest and worst.

You are my worst traits, also you continue without improvement. What you dreamed of in your youth, you still dream of now, an eon later. The stone you stumbled over when you were first born, you will stumble over that stone tomorrow.

You have given me my life and name, you have permitted me to hate you, you have given my hatred the vividness of suffering, you have made my hatred beautiful to you.

You have led me to build towers to your name, also to carve pictures to your self, also to form statues to your godhood. The tower, the picture, and the statue, they each fall free of you. They each do not stay with you. They have their

146

own names. I have named them, I have created them.

If I love you I will lose my youth. If I accept you I will become calm and slow. If I look on your face without spitting, I will become lost in the ages, I will become lost in time, I will vanish as all your creatures have vanished.

Let me forget you then. Let me love another.

Tell me of another I can love.

WOE, she sat with the youths, WOE told the youths of the Britons, WOE told them of the days when the Britons lived upon this island.

The Britons, WOE drove them out. My divine WOE, exiled to the center of the island, exiled to the top of the mountain by the rules and stories and books and words of the Britons, she drove them out, they are gone!

My WOE who has survived even Magellan and destroyed him, who has survived the Britons and smashed them! WOE, whose beauty is inexhaustible, whose desirability is equal to the strength of the word "love," must you be exiled by the rules of foreigners? Scorch their faces, fly into their eyes, stop their rule-giving mouths with earth!

You Britons who came in ships and cut the necklace off the body of WOE with a silver knife, your fate is known! You Britons who could not recognize the powerful woman, you who roared like dogs in a new language, your fate is known! Your story is already told, your story is over!

WOE is not weakened by laws. She turns laws to song. What can weaken her? She turns laws to song!

One who hears the stories told by Britons, that person is weak, that person is knowing, that person has no energy. That person is sure he is right, he can not move, he knows too much, he can not move.

One who hears the song of WOE, her song about the Britons, that person can move from age to youth. That person can move from wisdom to foolishness. That person can move from sleep to powerful wakefulness. Thank you WOE.

We sing about the Britons, we admire
their kicking and killing, we admire their strength
of chest to bellow, we admire their heart to drink
much alcohol.

We sing about Charles in white and red
cloth, red face and white teeth. Charles, Charles
is carved of the same rock as any holy thing. Any
rock by the great river, if splashed, gives out color
to show its gods, we say the name for wet rock
differently than dry rock. We sing of Britons,
they are dry rocks who wait and wait and wait for
rain.

Charles, Charles, I name you. I create you
again. I speak in your voice. I am your friend. I
offer you an alcohol. Here: I offer. But you must
obey me. You must drink what I am drinking.

We sing to create Charles again because he
is gone, he is gone. We sing goodbye to Charles,
we sing goodbye to the Britons. They have left us
because they hated us, they have left us because
they hated our island, they have left us because
the wood pulp ran out.

They, Britons, turned midday into dark-

degenerescence

ness. They turned each tree to pulp. They turned
TREE to PULP, a weaker god, a more general
god. They turned our words to Briton words,
general words, words that do not live in three
worlds.

WOE was guilty, who enriched the island.
WOE spoke the word "tree," she spoke the word
"pulp," she created the riches and the curse. Oh
do not sleep, WOE, do not dream of riches.
Dream of desert. Dream of desolation. Say "bar-
ren," say "empty." Watch the west, watch for the
ships. When they arrive, you must hide yourself,
WOE must hide herself. Go to the mountain! Go
on foot! Go and hide your daughters! Hide within
the mountain!

In exile sat WOE, hiding from the Britons, hiding within the mountain. She cried with
her seven daughters. The back of WOE's head
was wounded. Her face was burnt with adhering
tar. Her hair was matted with wax. She cried in
pain, she cried like a small child.

WOE who creates, WOE who created the
world, she has no one to ask, she has no one to
pray to. The Britons have destroyed TREE, and
renamed every object upon the island, renamed

every person upon the island, they have created
rules, created stories, history, they have laid books
upon the stones, books of words upon the stones.

The Britons called us savages. They
brought The Lord Your God, the invisible god of
the Britons. They taught us to forget WOE and to
pray to The Lord Your God.

WOE our queen, WOE our commander,
WOE our guru, WOE our general, WOE our
philosopher, WOE our angry elk, WOE our bitter
snake, our angry snake, WOE our silken boat,
WOE our dry ocean, we release you. WOE our
yellow jaundice, WOE our salted sugar, WOE
our fearful mountain, WOE our silent mother,
WOE our mysterious sister, we release you.
WOE, we release you.

I am released. The world worships The
Lord Your God.

The Lord Your God of the Britons, I
looked for him and I did not perceive him.

I perceived the nets, the dried eels, the feet
of the men, the flutes of the women, the beaks of
the birds, the voice of the earth, the dung of the

deer, the hair of my head, the moon.

But The Lord Your God I did not perceive him. He is the only god who does not exist. It is a great power. No word will call him. No prayer can find him. No shrine will trap him. He is free to destroy every thing.

I sang hymns to the Bull of the Sky. I said sing away, blow away, dry away, fall away, die away, so I can kill, so I can kill, so I can kill The Lord Your God!

The Bull of the Sky answered, saying: Who do the horns belong to? You will only stir up the water. You will make the Britons angry. You will fall into the dung.

The poison-plants all sang together, saying: You are too bitter for us, you will kill us with your song. Do not attempt to poison the Lord, he has no throat, he has no voice.

The distant island of Britain spoke slowly to me, saying Do I know you? Have we been introduced? You have me at a disadvantage. I do not know you. I will not acknowledge you. I do not dignify you. I do not see you. You are a wog.

You are a nigger. You are degenerated. You are the rot along the shore. You are the residue. You are the crust. You are not clean. You are impure. You have no emotions. You have no thoughts. You have no soul. You have no soul, you have no soul.

The Lord Your God, he did not answer, he did not speak, he did not thunder, he did not sing, he did not appear, he did not manifest. They say he is Love.

Daughters, said WOE, The Lord Your God can not give you his hand. I can give you my hand. Daughters, The Lord Your God can not smell your hair. I can smell your hair. Daughters, The Lord Your God can not play with you in the field, because The Lord Your God lives in Heaven Above, and he can not come here. I can come here and play with you in the field.

Daughters, The Lord Your God says he made all the things around you. He once walked on the earth, he once spoke to persons, he once appeared in the land. Today he can not do those things. He has lost the ability to do those things.

Daughters, you and I can do those things,

those simple things, but The Lord Your God can not do those things.

I can kiss you on the mouth! I can ride the tiger that bites away the moon! I can jump the ocean to the sun! I can act, I can act, The Lord Your God can not act!

That is what WOE said. WOE lives differently from persons of the island. They live on the earth, she lives in hymn. She scatters chaos, she brings floods, she causes terror and impotence among those who do not speak her language. WOE is a great singer of death, she brings the milk of death, she sets on fire the martyrs of Europa-speakers, she poisons their food, she howls. She hears what they say, she hears how they speak, she is bitter. She shouts and the earth rumbles. She crushes all humankind in her bowl, she mashes them in her bowl.

With her daughters she can speak her own words. Her daughters stay on the side of the mountain, making blue or yellow glass vessels beside a fire, they weep, they weep like the dead, but when they speak they speak the true language.

We of the island, we ignored the seven

daughters. We saw their purple or orange glass objects, we saw them, but we did not feel of them, we did not touch them, we did not look carefully. Even seaweed has a god, seaweed has an adventurous god, seaweed has seen much, but blue glass reflecting the moon, red glass changing the sun, glass was not very much to us. It was not useful, also it taught us nothing.

The Britons never cut down our trees. The Britons showed us how to cut them down most quickly. They filled ourselves with tree-cutting, so that we cut our own trees. Trees were destroyed into rolls of paper. Paper was cut, words were printed upon paper. The tree shouted from the paper, the white paper shouted. The smell of acid and wood can not drown the voice of a tree. But a word printed on paper is supreme, it can drown any voice. Paper money with words, it commanded even food. Paper books, they were more true than speech.

Paper books were piled around us. Paper books exhausted us. We learned to read the words, we learned to read the sentences, we learned to read the pages, we read, we read them all. Paper books are mighty, they are words carved for power, they destroy the mind, they destroy the voice.

To run, to smash, to shout, these are yours. Memory, arousal, wealth, these are yours. Heaven, grain, illnesses are yours. To raise the ocean to the sky, it is yours. A companion for love, a companion for sex, a companion for warfare, these are yours. A woman becomes a beast, a beast becomes a woman, a figurine becomes a god, ink becomes music. Admiration, renown, talent, applause are yours. To fly in the sky is yours, to become another sex is yours. In a paper book these things are yours.

We became the song we heard. We were the masters of the earth, but we became savages, we became degenerated, we became a race, we were a race. The picture in a paper book moves swiftly, it flashes across the eyes, it remains behind the eyes.

We learned that we were low, we learned that we were beasts, we learned that we were foul, we lived in the heat and brambles, we lived in the mud, we were shadows, we were shadows across civilization, we learned that our blood was dirty, we learned that our skin was filthy.

When we knew of the power and height
and purity of a Briton, we became aware of ourselves lower. We looked downwards, to see who
we were higher than, or purer than. We were
higher than dogs, though we always loved and
worshipped dogs. Now dogs were low, drinking
from puddles, wallowing, short in stature.

I am a savage, I am a low race.

I am of short stature compared to the
conquering Briton.

I am brown of skin, straight of hair, I am
beardless.

I am without much hair on the body, I
will show you, I will grin, it is a humiliation or
humility.

I am bashful. I am cold, not demonstrating
feeling. I do not have feeling in my heart.

I am broad of face, I am with ignoble small
nose, I am with flat animal eyebrows.

The cranium here, it leaves little room for
a soul.

All this I learned of my own self by reading real paper books, these things are true.

This is my blood makeup, my blood makeup. I am savage and nothing will change that.

To try to improve myself, it is the worst error. It will degenerate me further.

Already I should not have learned reading. Because I learned reading, I crave to drink matta, I crave to drink alcohol.

I was happy and golden when I could not read. The books tell me I am from a golden age, I have left behind the golden age. I am not now golden, I have lost myself. I am addicted to vicious practices.

I am degenerating. My very speech is lowering, it is lowering. I was happy and golden, now my organs are aging rapidly, they are gaining holes, they are like coral. I have degenerated organs. I have degenerated brain.

My instincts are lost. I should not have

spoken. I should climb a tree now. I can not even climb a tree.

I have learned all this from paper books. I am ruined.

The Lord Your God will not abide with me.

WOE will rise in me.

WOE is with me.

I have read the theories. We are not the worst island race. We are not the worst.

We cut trees. We cut trees for the Britons. Good. Other races are lazy, foul, degenerate, unintelligent. Others take pleasure and live without meaning. Others have time and waste it. We have no time at all.

I cut trees. I am greater than WOE, who only created trees. I make paper for a noble Briton, and the noble Briton takes the paper and writes on it. He writes "tree." He writes entire paper books. He names our island Mulatto. He names the other islands we slowly learned about.

He names savagery, nobility, words WOE
neglected to speak. He names Dyaks and Jakurs
and Fuegans.

The story in the paper book says Dyaks
lived on what we call "Island with Birds." The
story says Dyaks were great makers of music and
of painted things. With their mouths they could
talk words that called to gods we did not know,
and these gods could be seen dancing together
owing to the great talking ability of the Dyak.

The story says the Mulattans (ourself)
killed the Dyaks and burned their whole island
using fire, so that every color on their island was
become black color. The story says that we killed
these Dyaks, and brought them death. That is
what the book tells.

We do not know this story, also we do not
know the names of the words of the gods who
danced together.

The paper book tells the story of other
races: the Battaks who had the custom of amok-
running, also the Jakurs who had the custom of
suicide as a way of dance that tells story. Some
similar such. Yes it was dance to them. None of

these tribes is alive today. The names of these tribes make a black noise.

The least of all are called Fuegans.

These are the beastly of persons. They are storied for being low. They are below the orang. They are opposite to Britons.

I have read the paper books. Mr. Cook, Mr. Fitzroy, Mr. Wallin or Walloon, Mr. Darwin, Mr. Marx, all these famous experts believe the Fuegans are the most "low" and the most "base." Therefore they (Fuegans) are the original man or persons. This is spoken by paper books.

Men who tell stories, they tell of Fuegans, they are greatly funny. Laughter at the low Fuegans.

At night we dream in Fuegan. The dream words are Fuegan speech.

Fuegans move in our dreams, they are free. They have always youth, they are spirit. That is what our dreams think. Our dreams come from the thoughts of WOE.

In stories, Fuegans are stupid, dark-faced, weak, and they destroy themselves by accident. In a story when a Fuegan dies, nobody weeps.

In the smallest space within our head, Fuegans are kind, optimistical, prophetic, they are in love with the newness of the world.

In our speech, when we injure our bodies in error we say "fuego." That means we wish there were not these limits. We wish for a place without sharp points, we wish for love.

If drawing in the dirt with a stick, not thinking with thought, resting his senses, a person will draw Fuego. The shape of that place.

Inside the shape, a person will draw spiral. Spirit turns back as Fuegan speech does, it turns to one word, it rests and it turns back.

When I become smaller, more small, the words of paper books leave me.

When I become perfectly small, I am one voice, I speak one word. I am WOE.

In the island, in the mountain, in the rock

of the mountain is a dwelling.

Within the dwelling is a tiny space.

The space is the size of a word.

The space should be understood.

The space should be approached.

The space should be found.

All the words are in this one word. The word can not be pronounced. The word can not be spoken. WOE speaks this word. WOE pronounces this word.

If the word is spoken, if the word is written.

Then there is no word beast because there is no word human.

There is no word Fuegan, there is no word Briton.

There is no word angry, there is no word peace.

WOE is angry at the Briton, she loves the
Briton. She ignores the Briton, she is the Briton.
There does not exist such a thing as a Briton.
WOE prevents the Briton, she absorbs the Briton.

WOE speaks Briton, all words of Briton,
all Briton words, all enter the one space, all enter
the one word, all are renamed, all are created.

All paper books become empty, all paper
books are full of the one word.

All things and persons are in the one small
space, all breathe in one breath.

The Fuegan has skin like bird feathers.
The Fuegan is a bird, the Fuegan is a butterfly.

WOE has victory over the Briton. She has
forgotten the Briton. She has become the Briton.
She has forgotten the Briton. The Briton has left
the island. The Briton, who was on the island two
hundred of years, has left the island because
WOE loved him, WOE reduced him to a word,
WOE reduced him into every thing.

We are not good enough, we are not pure,

we can not follow WOE, we can not follow her thoughts. WOE who created daughters, while we created nobody, WOE who invented words while we only spoke words.

WOE whom WOE invented. WOE whom WOE made attractive with beauty. WOE who thinks with the speed of a war battle. WOE who feels more than heaven feels. WOE who is unknown, WOE who is ignored, beautiful and trembling WOE. My beloved WOE, keep providing! Let your words flow, keep speaking, keep singing! Do not forget us who neglect you. Do not forget words. Do not forget the three worlds you created. Let your words flow, keep speaking, keep singing!

The Britons have gone. We look at a fish, we say the Briton word "fish." We can not feel the fish.

WOE, remind us. Teach us how to see a fish. Teach us the word.

WOE, the gods are words and you are the book. The gods are words, you are the hymn. When you sing, you are the young man, you are the woman who waits in the footpath, you are the wife, you are the building, you are the king.

WOE, force the words to return to us. Use your power to make war on the words, let them obey us.

No person now remembers the way of praying to FISH to catch fish. When we try, we speak: FISH you are cheating me. FISH I am hungry! FISH you are a fraud! Why do you not feed me? You see me starving! FISH you are ugly, damn FISH!

In the old time, we could speak quietly and fish would jump to our laps. Today we remember the words of this prayer, but not the way of saying it. The way, we have lost the gift of the way. Now to speak it, it tastes like old fish.

WHEN A FISH LIVED IN ITS WORD

When a fish lived wetly in its word, then the sea was calm.

WHEN A FISH WAS AN HOMAGE

When a fish was an homage, statue, or totem of FISH, then the sea had depth.

WHEN A FISH SWAM IN AND OUT OF "FISH"

When a fish swimming in and out of its word "fish" stood in for all historical fish, then the sea had weight.

WHEN A FISH SPOKE OUT OF THE MOUTH OF **FISH**

When a fish speaking out of the mouth of god FISH stood in for all future fish, then the sea had the color of a sea.

WHEN THE WORD HAD THE MEAT
AND SAVOR OF FISH

When the word "fish" had the meat and savor of fish, then the sea tasted of the sea.

WHEN THE GOD GAVE THE SHIMMER

When the god FISH gave shimmer to a fish, then the sea had smell of a sea.

WHEN THE WORD SOUNDED FLEET

When the word "fish" sounded fleet, then the sea made sound of a sea.

WHEN THE FISH DEMANDED RESPECT

When the fish asked for respect out of its eyes, then the sea was good for serious work.

WHEN THE MAN WHO CAUGHT FISH
SPOKE TO FISH

When the man who speared the fish spoke to FISH, and ate fish while whispering "fish" then the sea was good for playing in.

WHEN FISH FED THE MAN

When the fish fed the man with more strength than only fish meat gives, then the sea could appear in dreams.

Let us go! Let us go there! Imbued with FISH let us enter the sea! The most beautiful seaweed, imbued with SEAWEED! The lovely water, full of WATER! We are milk of the sea. We are milk of the sun. If WOE will sing for us, we will be SONG.

WOE says: I have lost the gift to sing. I do not feel to sing.

WOE is without speech. We must return speech to her, we must return song to her. Words must return from where they have fled.

I will place my hand on her genitals, I will place my other hand on her mouth, bring my mouth close to her ear, take her ear into my mouth, the ear of WOE, take it into my mouth. This is the cleansing of speech.

My beautiful WOE, my creator, my silent one. You are not young, you have seen much, you have spoken much, you have sung every song you know. You are an alabaster statue, you are a faience statue, you are lovely and silent. My beloved, you have died in your voice, my sister, you have died.

Without words, without songs, the three worlds will be burnt, and the three worlds will be renamed.

Rain will not fall, as it will not be "rain," as it will not "fall." FALL will abandon the island, RAIN will forget the island.

Food will not create itself, even fish will be

abandoned by man. The fisher man will sit on land, he will eat dry leaves.

He will say, fish, fish are no longer important. Fish must not be thought of.

He will make a story, in place of food. He will make a story, in place of the objects of life.

He will say: In the past, in the black past, in the past, in the ignorant past, men prayed to fish and ate fish. But those fish then, they were not really fish. Those fish then, they had none of FISH in them.

He will say: Eating of fish, eating of fish does not need to be done. Eating of fish has already been done. Eating of fish does not need to be done again.

He will say: No one cares about fish, no one likes a fish. Catching fish is a nothing. Catching fish was always a nothing.

He will say: There is no FISH.

He will say: I am a fisher man. He will look at his belly.

The fish becomes a fish in a bucket, the sea becomes a bucket. The sea loses its savor. The sea loses smell. The sea makes no sound. The sea has no weight. The sea loses its depth. The sea loses its color. Fish become fish in a bucket, fish would not appear in dreams.

In the former times there was the fisher man. Then beside the fisher man, there were three, there were three. The builders who knew the voice in a piece of straw, who knew the god of clay, they knew how a word could be fixed so that it would remain. They were the makers of pots, the makers of huts, the makers of mosaics.

WOE who walked among them, who dwelt with them, who spoke to them in their sleep and watched their dreams, she kept company with each of the three. She, WOE, helped them learn their implements, their cutting tools, their styluses. She taught them the sand ritual, the echo-destroyer ritual, the vision ritual. She carried the light to them, she broke open the hard fruits, she aligned the snakes for the dance.

If there are no pots, there is no knowledge. If there are no mosaics, there is no spirit. If there are no huts, there is no religion. Do not worship the name of WOE and neglect the pot on the floor, it holds rain, it keeps the breath in your voice, it is stronger than the name of WOE. Do not worship the name of WOE and neglect the mosaic tile on your wall, it contains the word in a picture, the word will last longer than the breath in your voice, it is stronger than the name of WOE. Do not worship the name of WOE and neglect the hut you live in, it preserves your body, it rescues the breath in your voice from storms and death, it is stronger than the name of WOE.

There is no god without the speck of dirt on the wall. There is no spirit without the game persons play with cowrie shells. There is no belief without the cooked potato. There is no mystery without the ordinary sea-bird.

The hut maker. For one who makes huts, the god is not in the earth, it is in the hut. For one who makes huts, the anti-god is not in the sky, it is in the hut, it is of the hut.

In the past, in the days of the past, all persons made their own huts. Later we built stone houses for the Britons and the Europas. But, to build a stone house for ourselves, we lost the desire and gift and knack or facility and skill and easy knowing of stone house building.

WOE said: Hut maker, may you be one who pleases himself, may you be a son without a mother, may you prosper without grain or cattle. May you not know the name of Briton or Mulattan. May you have no name. May you do work without a name.

That is what WOE said.

Huts rise slowly. A hut takes time to build it. During this time, the hut maker believes he will not be able to finish hut. He dreams of a complete hut that suddenly falls down.

On the island are many crippled huts. The hut maker gives up partway, then finishes badly, he does not care. These huts have gods without tongues, without bones or eyesight. They burn often.

On the island are many huts that were not begun. You think of a hut and you have a thought hut. In these huts nothing happens, no life is there. They degenerate by growing bigger in the mind. They have no doors.

WOE said, make huts.

The hut maker called that a curse. He said furious words. He made a hut in fury, in a single motion, like the blow of an axe.

WOE, I have built you a home! I have flattened the ground and demolished the trees, I have made a plot, I have built up the fragile clay, I have dug out gutters, I have planted poles, I have covered walls with woven roots. In this hut the honey is aromatic, the cedar posts are aromatic. There is beer, incense, cakes, and a door to close, a door to bolt you in.

Stay here with your seven daughters. Let your daughters not come to me in the night, let them not speak gently to me, let them lie on their bellies and hide their faces behind the walls I have built. WOE, if you speak new words, if you create new gods, if you continue the change that destroys, then behind these walls no one will hear your words. Your changes will be uncreated, time will not kill its citizens, the island will not flood, the weather will not change, new persons and deer and boars will not be born, the earth can rest as long as you are locked here. Lock yourself here.

Pay me for my work. I ask for praise, I ask for gold.

WOE and her seven daughters praised the hut maker who did not like to be named, they paid him in gold they created with their mouths, but they did not live in his hut with thick walls and a door-bolt. They returned to the cedar forest within one moment, leaving him alone.

He lived there. He was renamed in that hut. He was joyful. He made huts for others, for payment. Clouds of weakness came to him. He slept, instead of preparing the mud. He fell asleep, instead of flattening the ground. He fell asleep, instead of removing rocks, cutting vines, digging out roots.

He did nothing, instead of something.

Instead of building huts, he dreamed of building huts.

The hut of weakness, he dreamed of building it.

The hut of anger, he dreamed of building it.

The hut of ignorance, he dreamed of building it.

The hut of surety, he dreamed of building it.

The hut of trying to please, he dreamed of building it.

The hut of energy, he dreamed of building it.

The hut of old age, he dreamed of building it.

He did nothing. He felt proud. Vividly he saw a circle of persons surround him to praise him. He felt strong. Vividly he saw a circle of persons gift him with small golden houses and hammered funeral jewelry.

He had no name. He grasped air, he held air, he breathed in air, air rose to his mind, he sang without breath, he sang without sound.

The few huts he built, they stood well. No one thought of the builder of the huts. He was not known, he was forgotten, he was not remembered.

The mosaic maker. WOE said: A picture in tiles of a man ablaze, that is a man ablaze. Only the spirit to speak those two words together, "man," "blaze," only that spirit is needed.

The mosaic maker in youth, the mosaic maker in his former, lost years, was a timely rain that floods heaven with joy. He was a sweet dragonfruit, red as flesh. He was the jewelry of a great king. He was a goddess atop a polished stone. He was a drinking cup filled with matta. He was honey on the tongue of a joyful husband. He was the spark in the mind when words contend.

He arranged tiles into scenes of discomfort and dismay. He would not explain his tiles. He decorated every wall.

He shows in tile the face of the man who tells lies.

He shows in tile the wishes of a dog on the footpath.

He shows in tile the fish that knows it is netted.

He shows in tile the man whose wife shouts at him.

He shows in tile the absence of the beloved.

These tiles he made when young. In the
present, this mosaic maker is old, he is old. He
lets nobody see inside his hut.

In the morning he feels new air and hears
the birds sound, he can not rise from bed as he is
very old.

He hears persons walk to the river for
water. He hears a fool laugh. He hears a person
throw a rock at a tree.

He is angry. He is an old person. He is the
lightning far off. He is a flame at noon. With
anger, he can rise from his bed.

The tiles he makes are not for us. Even
WOE does not see into his eyes. Even WOE does
not know his purpose. He is too old, he does not
think in words.

His tiles are not tiles, today. They are
implements, shakers, foot-paintings, bird-imper-
sonators, songs, sand-rituals, self-cleansings, self-

anointment with filth, hymns, repetitions, forgetting-rituals, divinations by mongrels.

Despite the famous incidents regarding his wife and daughter, he is a wise man, he feels all the tiles are depicting of his serenity.

He believes that whoever is serene, that person has won victory.

If any person stop him on the footpath, he will shout at them in unknown words. If a person should call him venerable master, he will shout and curse them.

He gave his name away to a stone, then he threw the stone into the air.

He made tiles that were letter forms, he made pictures of words, they were not a book.

When his death comes, he will burn his own hut, using matches and paraffin. His mosaics will crack and melt and will not be seen, they will not speak of inner peace or serenity to any other person. They are not a story, not a story. They will carry his body with them.

The potter. WOE has seen a potter die on the island.

The potter, the word "potter" created him, WOE bore him up by his name. He made the same pot again and again, he filled the land with pots until he saw that all pots break. He asked: Why should I produce breakables. This is the same as working hard to create broken bits of pot. That is what he said. When his hair turned white, he changed his name so it would be clear what had happened to him.

With his new name, he could only lie back and speak of his fears. He smiled all the time. This is what he said: Dearest one, stay away from the ocean. Do not touch it! I remember I was almost drowned. The ocean took me away and killed me, almost so. That was sixty-two years ago. Remember that and do not forget my words.

I also was almost killed once more by the falling of a coconut. I will not eat coconut even today. You must not eat coconut. That occurrence was sixty-eight years ago.

That was the speech of the first potter.

He defended his house against coconuts, by amulets. He only drank water after shouting at it, in case it drown him.

He planned to poison all trees that give coconut, also he planned to empty the ocean. OCEAN and COCONUT both knew this man. They did not strike at him. They saw that he was old, deteriorating, foolish, gray, weak, maundering, weeping, incapable, confused, blind, deaf, trembling, drooling, toothless, sexless. They did not strike at him. They saw that he could not make pots, he could no longer make pots. They did not strike him down.

He awoke. He drank matta. He drank matta until he felt POT enter his arms.

The god was trapped in his arms. His idea of a pot became gigantic. He saw a pot to make persons weep and worship.

He was the god POT but he could not move.

When young he slammed the clay. When young he made a cup and a bowl and a pot like a fist smashing. When young he laughed. He threw pots out of himself. His pots had energy and unkindness.

Later when old he did not feel he should harm the clay. The clay has its own preference. The clay is dead and wishes to be undisturbed.

He drank matta so he would be wise. Wisdom happens to old men, he said. Am I old? Wisdom is tragic, it happens to the old. With wisdom, you say a thing just because it is true. You can not have a new moment, you can not change, you can not destroy, with wisdom. The pot maker said all this. He said: Stupidity is better. I am going to become more stupid.

The pot maker said: Do I drink matta well, or only dutifully? I ask because I am unsure of myself. I am unsure because I am still young, still young.

The pot maker observed degeneration among aging birds.

On an evil day our pot maker died, we were without pots. He asked, do I repeat myself? He said, old men repeat themselves. He asked, Am I old? and he died.

Because we live on an island, life has ended. We are like stone statues. Every rock has been seen, every tree has been seen. All stories are told, the stories are lost to telling. Every person wishes to be elsewhere. Also, every person is afraid to enter a boat and leave.

The red rat stays in its nest, it will not come out for food. The red rat looks out at the food. It is impossible to come out of this nest, coming out of a nest can not be done by any rat. Priorly, but not now.

The crayfish eggs do not hatch.

The tree has a hole. A grub crawls around the circle of the hole, grub does not go into hole, grub does not go out of hole.

The pig sees its face in the eye of the water of the pond. The pig then fails to eat or drink.

Persons die, they stop moving. WOE, all persons you created will die. WOE, all your seven daughters, they will depart. WOE, what have you created? The island dies, your island dies.

In the eon to come, no WOE will be created. The world will be, but without the person or thing or word in it.

We determined to prevent change and new incidents.

We named "time" from our mouths in ceremony. We did speak the word "time" and TIME came then. We emboxed TIME and killed the box with arrows, and we buried this box.

We covered the Greater Swastika River with bamboo and thatching. We covered the Lesser Swastika River with bamboo and thatching.

No flowing could occur.

Yet a man shouted at his wife, then they did not speak together after that, there was a change. A stone fell off the highest hill and rolled into the water, it did not rise back, there was a change.

WOE, return back our huts and our clothing. Move back all plants and trees. Make this the exact island it was before Magellan came. Kill all words since that day. It is reckless to kill words, since they live in the mind, and they live in sleep. But WOE can kill a word, such that it was never spoken and never known.

We will forget our newer tools and fish-hooks and looms. We will think of WOE and nothing else, and become timeless persons. We will not age, we will not die.

WOE, do this.

WOE, today a man died of belly difficulty, and another died because he was too old. That is terrible, it is a story, it will not cease.

We will wait for WOE. She has hidden herself inside a root of a water plant, none can find her. We will only sit, we will tell no stories. What if we tell a story, and it comes out newly?

WOE, we ask you, wipe our names away, we ask you, make us unborn. We are not good, we were never good. Your creation is an error. We have disappointed you. We have betrayed you.

Mashed roots are our food, they all are stale. All seaweeds have a rotting flavor. River water is brown. Animals are silent. The cliff beside the beach, the rock cliff, the rock comes away under the hand. The cliff is full of holes, the rock has no weight. If you throw the rock at a man, he laughs.

The mist-tree or cloud-tree, it is unliving. It never gives out with hues. Nor does it change by the season. It has rotted in place, TREE is not present there.

Small cages and traps for pigs are in piles, tangled. Nobody uses them, they are un-thought-of.

Plough parts, knives, the use of them is not remembered. Persons eat what grows there and there. Every person grows thinner.

Each day we lose one word more. WOE, watch over us. We stop speaking of metal, or music, or boats, we forget them. Then they forget us and they leave us forever. WOE, watch over us.

WOE, if you are empty, do not tell us. WOE, greatest god, if your name is empty, if you do not exist, then do not tell us.

We will worship she-who-is-not, she-who-is-not will free us. We adore the lotus feet of WOE who gives us nothing, the only name with perfect emptiness. WOE, we do not see you, thank you. WOE, take us into your non-existence.

For a man, for our men, the man is not a man, the phallus has lost its memory. MAN leaves him. The woman keeps her own name and "woman." But the man has no name, because his phallus has lost its memory.

None of the men have a phallus that remembers. A woman will do all she can, she will name a thousand names to the phallus, she will perform rituals to the phallus, she will create new songs and sing them to the phallus.

The man will not speak. He has no words inside. Thereby no children are born to the island.

In the ancient times, in the time of the past, banquets were eaten. Old stories tell of food, old stories tell of great waste of cooking and mashing, the banquet. These are not now eaten, these are not now cooked, these are not now

known. Go, put the yoke around your neck, think
of lost things. Remember names whose sound is
lost. Eat the name of the air, eat the name of no
name, try to eat your fill.

Men tell stories of banquets that lasted
many days. You will never see such food. You
will die without knowing pleasure of food. After
you die, you will see only the hidden names of
food, and the hidden appearance of food. You will
talk to the god FOOD but you will receive no
reply.

Even after death you will remember the
story of women who chop and mix for seventy
days to produce the food shaped like a puff of
silver, tasting of every good food at once, rising as
you eat it, rising to the mind.

We eat only what grows by itself. We eat
young bamboo.

Young bamboo grows up again every
place. WOE, how does it come back? When I eat
it, it is soft. It is young.

Yoke yourself, wish, wish to live in an old
story. On this island "matta" is the name of the

alcohol drink. The word has not changed in a thousand of years, but the drink has changed.

Drinking of the legendary matta, it made expansion, dreaming, flying, love, wishes, a full heart, a completed spirit.

The god HORIZON was always drunk on matta, lying there, lying flat within the sight of all persons, generous to the sea and sky.

Briton liquor, that was never favored among the persons of the island, it caused loss and nightmare, as when you are hit on the head with a stone. But during the Briton time, real matta-making was forgotten.

Drink today's matta and you will feel frightened. You are calling a god who is dead, and drinking a drink without a god.

Today pigfruits are thrown in a bucket of water, spat on, and stirred once. After two weeks it is remembered and drunk sour from the bucket. We drink, we drink. In the sky there is the bird of paradise, in the earth there is the iron god and the stone god. But lying on the island we are embar-rassed. What are we, we are degenerated at birth.

What are we, we are the baby born without a head. We are the baby born without a skin.

Our race was not created by a goddess. Our race was founded by brainless giants. Our race was created by scheming cripples. Our fathers traveled the island wearing no clothing, our fathers ate each other. They ran among each other naked, the taste of flesh rose up.

Today we look down as we walk. Today we do not look in each other's faces. We are clothed, we eat roots but this is not progress. We are angry, we are shy, we are humiliated, we have low energy, we have little life. We are old.

There is no WOE, there is no goddess. There is no smoke that brings words out of the mouth of the dead.

Our king is the last king. One thousand of years his fathers were king. He will be the last.

His fathers did magic. Also our king could do magic when he was young. He could stab a person across space and time. He also did not care who he stabbed.

You were making sex in the forest, and found the iron blade in your stomach. The knife was sent to you from a year hence. Or from before your birth. The knife, it came to you out of the sky, or it came to you out of a stone. It came from your kindness and grace, or it came from your evil deeds. There was a real knife in you. The king did not mind if you died. He was a great worker of magic.

He was our king. He shined in water. He was the mind of the fetus. He held apart the edges of the sea.

The king, our king, he made his second wife go mad. He made her to see her head inside a bell, ringing it.

The king, our king, he made the most sage and most good man on the island begin to eat without cease. Ate and ate because he thought food was become truth.

Our king when young, he was tallest person of the island. Today he the most short person. All persons of the past are giant, WOE is infinitely taller than her seven daughters, all island persons of now are invisibly short.

Now our king is more old than any person. He can do no magic. But he can see magic.

He is short and old. He is limited but he sees the unlimited.

He walks on the island, he looks at our fates. He sees ancient persons. He sees the ancient island.

He believes he is young and WOE is young and island is young. He shouts at Magellan, he shouts at Pigafetta and the Prophet Muhammad, he shouts at Shiva and at the child Jesus.

He warns us all against blood pollution. He calls us all enlightened, he speaks of revelations.

We wish to understand our king, we wish to follow him. But we are not advanced enough to try. He walks beyond our seeing, he sees beyond our seeing.

We cry, we kiss him, we ask him to explain. He looks at us, and sees young strong persons instead of who we are. He tells us we are great and able, he tells us we have the power to do any thing, and we beat our heads and weep.

King, why do you not say your revelations so we can understand. Why do you not say your revelations in the language of your people?

He replies: Such things can not be said in the language of the people.

Let us die if we are going to die. Pour beer and wine from the jars, let us destroy our younger names, let us give away the names we had when young. Now we are tired, we can not follow a king, we can not love our women, we can not find our way, we have lost WOE. We heard WOE speak, we saw her walk with us. But we would not wed her daughters, and she left us.

Let us do nothing but drink beer from the vat. We want to feel wonderful. We want to die, we want to clothe our deaths in laughing.

The air now is like air just before the monsoon. When you breathe, the air calls itself "air," it will not be renamed by BREATH into "breath." We will not breathe this air. We will not remember how beautiful we used to be. We will not remember the jokes we made. We will not remember the stories we told. We will not remember the thighs of the young woman. We will not remember the thighs of the young man. We will not remember love words spoken to us. We pour the wine over brick, we pour the wine through stones. We will put our young names under stones, we will not continue to wait.

We will not wait for ourselves to be strong again. We will not wait for anybody to fall in love with us. We will not try to sing poetry. We will wait for dreams in our sleep to tell us what to do.

We will scratch lines in the dirt under the tree. We will push stones with our feet. We will lie down all the time. We will not recite another hymn. We will not draw WOE's body in berry juice on the side of the cliff. When hungry, we will fill our mouths with pleas. We will plead: Let me alone. We will plead: Forget me. Our goats are free, our sheep are free, our pigs are free. If the pigs round us up and herd us, we will sit in a pen, we will not try to escape. We will take what food the pigs feed us.

WOE, come.

WOE, tell us. Show us.

We are not only this. Tell us, if we are only this. Are we only this? Tell us.

I am WOE. I have not disappeared.

I hear your dreams. I talk to your dreams. In your sleep I convince you. In your sleep I strengthen you.

When you stoned the prostitute to death, you stoned me. When you pursued excessive work in the time of the Britons, you offended my creation. When you drank beer and matta, you consumed the island. The island will sink away. The water will drink you. You will be ornaments for coral. You will be fed on salt. You will be content with namelessness.

That is true. That is true because you do not know it is not true. This is not an island, if you knew. This is the world, if you knew. This is not going to die or sink, if you knew.

Here, the shell of a conch. The shell has beauty more than a pot or picture painting. Conch

of infinite ancestry is held as ever by god SHELL.
SHELL is here. If every shell in the world is
destroyed in a battle of the shells against the sea,
SHELL is here. "Shell" can make shells in infini-
tude by speaking itself. "Shell" is a true word.
"Shell" is one word of the unknown story. The
unknown story is a million million words in
length. It, story, does not exist without this one
shell.

That is the end of the words of WOE. We
do not understand them.

We cry out against ourselves in the mountains. We wear garments of mourning for ourselves. We diminish our own names. We pursue
the word for strength, we speak the word for
strength, that word dies in our mouths. We do
not know how to call STRENGTH to appear.

What was WOE speaking? Words about a
shell. We try to worship shells, empty shells. We
crush shells like malt and swallow them. We wait
to become young, bright, strong, easy in strength,
full with pleasure, full with ability.

When we failed to marry our young men
to the seven daughters of WOE, was that our

error? Her daughters are ugly, like ripped sacks, like crushed wet reeds. WOE can not require this sacrifice. We will smother, we will drown, do not make us marry the wretched daughters, the seven wretched makers of deformed glass bowls, disfigured glass bowls, lopsided blue glass bowls. Let the seven live among their bowls, let the seven sleep with blue bowls. We can not marry women we can not understand.

We sew a flag with Briton words and fly it, it reads ADVANCE IS DESCEND.

None understood that WOE was standing on the edge of the water. None understood that WOE was weighing two sounds with her hearing. None understood that WOE was sorrowful when we danced, that WOE was uncertain when we shouted prayers.

She is standing on the edge of water at night. Because she has not spoken, she is pure of all music, she hears ocean waves as music, she hears all the notes. WOE knows the names of all the notes.

To play Dha Ni Dha on the clay flute is not of music unless the playing person inwardly speaks "Dha Ni Dha," the names of the sounds. No sound can occur without WOE knowing its several names in words.

She has seven daughters. She is alive. Hence she will have her eighth daughter now. What else is there for her?

She plays a note on the clay flute. She is too tired to think of the name of the note. She is too old to think what scale it is in. She is too lonely to protect herself from this note.

A sound without a name, it can cut stone, it can melt sand. Music is prior to words, this note is prior to music.

Should she play clay flute music to the persons, so they can dance? The clay in their bodies dances to the clay of the flute. They do not hear the note, they hear the clay. Should she play music impossible to dance to, so they can hear the notes?

The unbeliever will be rewarded. The uncertain person will be rewarded. The believer will suffer.

WOE, greatly wise, full of kindness, worthy of praise, stood on the sand, her foot was not pressed onto the neck of any being on earth. Praise of WOE was rare, she did not demand praise, she did not demand belief. The unbelievers live the free lives. WOE fashioned seven daughters for the world, she could not fashion an eighth daughter. She could not demand praise, but she could not continue without praise.

Some words are created by food you eat. If you eat another food you will speak a different word. To speak much, eat every food.

WOE ceased to eat all foods except the smashed paste of walnuts. No words come from a smashed paste, except for the names of the dead, also the words for need.

When alone, WOE played flute for herself as she preferred, without song. Each toot or sound was a body without a name. In one sound you hear the bottom of her feet. In one sound is her forehead. When she played and listened, she would cry quietly. But her daughters felt they were hearing the middle of a song too long to remember.

Flute blowing is for a purpose, as making a pot or hut. This purpose was not discovered in the time of WOE. It has not been discovered still. WOE can not tell the purpose for her flute.

Other musics on the island are useful.

The seven daughters sing Kaludi songs. The Kaludi singer is useful, she must weep over the death of an elder. She will sing weeping for a good or bad elder equally.

The seven daughters sing to WOE. They sing: You have grown weaker. If only you were young again.

The Kaludi song gives happiness to the dead. It pleases dead ones to be flattered. If we fail to sing it, if we fail to give happiness to the dead, then at a later time, when we are dead, we will not expect happiness then, we will hear no flattering song.

WOE looks outside the island. Every thing outside the island is confused and causes disturbance.

WOE looks upon the island. Every thing

on the island is confused and causes disturbance.

WOE heard the song her daughters sang to her. She did not look at her daughters. She looked at the ocean, she said "ocean" because this was the first time she knew what it was.

When she said "ocean" she saw the ocean, she saw the moving of seaweeds and grabbing-plants, she saw each wave in every place it waves, she saw the ocean surround the earth as a hand on a ball.

WOE said "ocean." She saw the darkness of every inch under ocean. She felt the currents in every place, she felt how the ocean feels the moon.

The ocean feels the winds, it rises, it rains into itself. It is the water in the air, it is the air. It rains into the earth and plants eat it, persons eat it, they weep it out, it returns in rivers. WOE saw this in the instant of the word.

Then, this is what she saw: she saw the sun move in the sky one small movement. Then all of these things changed and were otherwise.

"Ocean" was a larger word than WOE
could think at this time. The sun moved again.
All other words, she saw them changing, she saw
all other words too large to speak.

The days have multiplied, no salvation has
come for this island or its creator. The persons of
the island sit and wait. Disbelieving their creator,
they call out: Let us sail away, let us sail away!
They possess boats with sails for fishing, small
log-canoes, small flat-boats, also barges. Yet they
do not enter these, they do not row these, they do
not sail these, they do not go onto the water. They
sit still on the earth, they call: Let us sail away!

The seven daughters of WOE, the seven
created by WOE, the seven who have died, they
make blue glass things because there is no need
for blue glass things. There is no reason for the
seven daughters to exist. They do not escape, they
do not swim, they do not float away in boats.
They sit on the earth, they call out: Let us sail
away! Let us float away! Let us sail away with
you, our mother!

WOE, who spoke the one hundred thousand of words, she is mute. WOE, who made all
things, if she closes her eyes she sees Briton

things, Europa things. WOE who crossed from the other world, WOE who leapt from the other world, she has no strength in her thighs. She has no strength in her hips. She says without speaking: No one sails with me.

WOE who made all relationships and laws, she has forgotten laws, she lives by the laws of others, she obeys the past laws, she does what is expected of a serf, she does what is expected of a slave. She pulls her boat with her own hands, she drags her own boat down to the sea. No one helps her, no one sees her.

When she created the world, no one saw. When she gave out with the seven, no one saw, no one looked. The waters of the mist-tree are not to be tasted again. The dragonfruit, the dates from the palm tree, the yellow roots soaked in brine, they are not to be tasted again.

The clay flute is full of the songs of others, it is heavy to lift. The ears with which she hears the sea, they are full of the voices of others, they are full of foreign words and laws. The persons of the island produce no children now. The sheep of the island grow no wool. Why should she not sail?

The air is full of stories, words are all locked into chains of words, words are locked together, words can not be separated, words can not be rearranged, words can not be spoken truly. Why should she not sail away?

She who brought flocks of birds together across the sky, she who controlled the flight of birds, she has forgotten how. She has lost the ability to make sea waves come in varying heights. She has forgotten how to make a man walk along a path and feel inwardly. She has lost the ability to make women talk together in wonderment. She has forgotten, she has lost the ability. Why should she not sail away?

The reasons for things, she has forgotten. The answers to questions, she has forgotten. The solace of speech, she has forgotten. The knowing of an opinion, she has forgotten. The beauty of a silence, she has forgotten. What to do with time, she has forgotten. Love of strangers, she has forgotten. Confessing errors, she has forgotten. Asking a question, she has forgotten. The order of events, she has forgotten. The color of the monkfish, she has forgotten. Where to walk now, she has forgotten. The pleasure of energy, she has forgotten. The sound of voices, she has forgotten. Every thing she used to know, she has forgotten. Why should she not sail away?

At present she is dragging her boat to the sea, she is dragging her own boat down to the sea.

I see her, I see WOE, I see the trees that refuse to make further leaves. I see her, I see the trees that let their bark fall down. I see her, I see the trees that cover themselves in dirt.

Water of the ocean, I see it become dry, though it is also water. The ocean no longer makes sounds, the waves give up, the waves sit still. The waves sit on the ocean like women with their heads bowed.

The birds died while flying through the air. After they died, they fell in the ocean.

The fish tried to eat the birds that fell there, so that the fish also died.

The fire is cold and black in color, it stops flicker, it glares.

The wind is gone, it makes only the sound

of groan or low roar of cheerlessness.

No person moves. The men who catch fish, they lie on the floor of their boats, they dream of death.

A voice comes from the earth, it says *That is true*.

I speak to the earth, saying:

I am WOE's eighth daughter. Do for me what you have done for others. Make me to be born, give me animal appearance.

WOE will not create me, WOE refuses to create me, loneliness is making my death, oh god of my body which is not.

Earth, let me abandon my non-state, give me life so that I can live and die. When you stamp my face in the sky, I will find my name, I will be dead, and I will praise you.

Those were the remarks of the eighth daughter of WOE.

She is WOE's daughter who is not born.

She said to me, How is it you see me? Nobody sees me, nobody hears me.

I told her this: Should I pretend I can not see you, should I pretend I can not hear you? You are strange to say so. You are as strange as your mother, you are as strange as your sisters.

I asked her to tell me why her mother WOE is going away, why she is sailing away.

She said: It is because she will do anything to play the flute.

Is it possible WOE is like that? What is a flute noise so worth?

She said: It has the same worth as any thing. It has the same worth as a person. It has the same worth as a god. A sound, a person, a god, all of them go away. All of them first fail, and then go away.

That was the reply of the eighth daughter of WOE.

WOE is taking her boat, she is floating away within her boat. When disease rained from the sky, WOE was the air. When orchids were discovered, she was the odor. When war began, she was the soldier. When a banquet of barley grass and nuts and every kind of food was begun, she was the flesh of the grain. When it was time to allow her daughters to die, she was the hand that withheld honey and milk from their mouths. When pictures appeared in the minds of sleeping persons, she was the face that told them they could fly. When air was blown through a flute, she was the hymn, she was the requiem.

When nothing appeared, when the rain did not fall, when the food did not grow, when all the boats sank, when the astronomer forgot his craft, when the painter's hands shook, when there was no dream in sleep, when there was no sleep after the meal, when there was no food to eat, when copulation failed, when the child could not be born, when the names of the dead were forgotten, then she was there, she was the cause, hers was the blame.

She should depart, she should sail away.

She hangs the cloth on the mast, she ties it back. She blows through her flute. Her note is heard by all names, her note is heard by all ob-

jects, her note is heard by all the gods. Every
thing she does is known by the three worlds.
Every word she says is heard by the three worlds.
She does not know it. Her hair is spread across
the horizon, if she only knew. Her eyes cover the
waters like silk, if she knew. If she knew, she has
all power, she has all force, she has truth, she is
the name, she is the god, if she knew.

She sails. She is gone from the sight of the
island. She travels seven earshots away from the
island. She is not disappeared, she is on her boat.
She exists. She can not vanish until she vanishes.
She still sees herself.

We of the island have lost her to ourselves.
Her name has changed. She became old and
changed her name. Even the god WOE dies with
the name.

We do not know her name now. We are
the creation of a destroyed person. It is the same
as if WOE were burnt in the flames, and her
resulting bones were held overhead and thrown
with both arms into the sea.

The new woman, her hair is white, from
the loss of a name. The god departs and takes the

color. She has sailed, her bones weigh nothing.

She says: I am on the boat.

I am alive. How does this be?

I am alive because I am not very afraid.

I have lost my name. My boat is becalmed.

The wind is stopped. The wind that carried words into our world is stopped. The wind that carried the thumb-sized souls into the heart of every name is stopped. The wind that pushed my name into my body, it is stopped. The wind that carried words out of my chest into the air, it is stopped. The wind that colors thoughts silver is stopped. The wind that makes all persons know the same things, that wind has stopped. The wind has stopped blowing, the wind has lost its name to "air," the wind is only air.

The bottom of my boat holds me from death by drowning, the bottom of my small boat.

I cut my palm with the sharp black stone, but the blood on my hand does not dry. There is no wind, so the blood does not dry, therefore no omen is created and I do not know the truth.

I cut my face with the sharp black stone, but the blood on my face does not dry. There is no wind, so the blood does not dry, therefore no omen is created and I do not know the truth.

I cut my belly with the sharp black stone, but the blood on my belly does not dry. There is no wind, so the blood does not dry, therefore no omen is created and I do not know the truth.

When the truth comes, there will be blood every place.

The sky is atop me, the sky is atop WOE, the sky is atop the woman who was WOE.

The earth is bright, even if I call it the sea. The sea is filled with voices even if I call it fire.

I can see things without knowing their names. Words and names have left me, alongside of the word for me, the name for me.

When I go into the water, there will be no word for that.

When I swim down, there will be no word for that.

What will I be when I do not see, what will I be when I do not name things, what will I be when I do not make hymns? What will I be when the island I created is without me? What will I be when the island I created sinks in the ocean? I will be without a name, and my condition will be without a name.

These are remarks made by the old woman who was previously WOE.

The boat stops to move, the boat stays unmoving upon the water. The boat has not moved, because it has no wind, it has no impelling force of wind.

When the old woman was becalmed, her cry reached every region of the sky. Her voice carried fire, her voice carried creation, her voice made the grasses of the earth crouch in the dust, the crying of her voice made fire weep water.

I will sweep everything away. That is the cry of the old woman.

I shall die, I shall be a stone, I shall be a vile plant, I shall be a fungus, I shall be scum on the water, I shall be residue. That is the cry of the old woman.

I will die without creating even a speck. I will die without creating even a nameless speck. What was this for?

I will live in the sky, in the place of orphans. The sky place of mute persons, the sky place of extraneous beings, the place of forgotten unnamed beings. What was this for?

This is what the old woman said.

She left the boat, she entered the water with her own body.

She can swim, if she knew. She can play songs on her flute, if she knew. She does not know, so that she will dive down until she stops. Let her death be death. Let there be no Briton heaven with musical harps. Let there be no Turkic hell with reciting of her errors, she knows her errors. Let there be no fame, no white-colored fame. Let the sea be dark and without sound, let the sea say nothing to her to remind her of the days she believed she was the creator of the universe. Wild sea with green thighs, rise up and take, rise up from the place of waiting, you who have always waited.

The sea said to the island, is this woman not WOE, is she not your priestess?

The island said, we are low, we are ignorant. Ask the Britons.

The sea said to the Britons, is this woman not WOE, creator of the greater world, namer of the sea and sky, creator of the three worlds?

The Britons answered, she is not known to us. She is not important. She is small.

The sea said to the Britons: Look, here is the great WOE, the creator WOE.

The Britons said, if she were the creator, would we not know it? Would we not feel fear at her name? Would we not be on our knees in the dust to her? Would we not propitiate her with gold and burnt cattle? Would we not carve her name and image onto our metal slabs? Would we not write her life in a thousand books? Then they said:

We have ignored her since the beginning of time. Should she not be bitterly angry, if she is the great one? Should she not fill our rivers with stones? Should she not strike our beautiful women with sores? If she is the creator, should she not cast down our multitudes, and salt our fields, and sink our island of Europa? Then they said:

Let her destroy us now, if she is great.

Let her show her power. Let her prove she is the god. Let her change our hearts. She is the creator, then let her change our hearts. Then they said:

She does not exist. Your goddess, she does not exist. Your creator, she is smaller than the smallest thing. Our friends do not know her. Our wise men do not mention her. Our politicians do not praise her. Our commoners do not reach out for her. Then they said:

We have not seen her in our gatherings. We have not seen her among the famous. We have not seen her among our images. She is not of our people. She is not interesting for us.

That is what the Britons said.

When she dives down, never to rise again, she will disappear from the world of names. She will not have a body to be "she," she will not have a body to be a "body," she will not have "have." She will lie down under the water and will not rise again.

She who spoke will never speak again. She who created will never create again. She who destroys her self will never destroy more. She will lie under the water and never rise again.

She will be unable to swim, she will be unable to sing, she will be unable to flute, she will be unable to sigh and complain.

She will not feel neglected, she will not feel ignored, she will not feel un-worshipped, she will not be filled with bitterness. She will not bitterly watch images of persons in her mind. She will not watch images of persons doing chores and failing to bow to her, WOE. She will not hear images of persons talking and not talking about her, WOE. She will not imagine every surface of the world or island, and stare at each surface, and see that her name is not engraved there, WOE.

Instead she will be in the solitary place without images. She will be in the deer-trap, where no escape is possible. Her mind can not escape and her voice can not escape, her will can not escape and her name can not escape. Her seven daughters are dead, they can not escape, they are only images, they live only within her, she is the trap, she will not escape.

Even under the water she will be wrong, she will be in error. She will lie still, yet she will think she is in penance, she will think she is in sacrifice. She will think: I will stay here for two years, and I will purify my heart, and I will not see the sky, and after that time, I will speak every word in the universe, and I will create the world from nothing, I will be present when the truth is created, I will create the truth, and this time I will put the words in the best order. So each god's name is harmonious with the next god's name. The gods are kind and calm. I will speak the names, the result will be calm and harmony.

That is what she will think. But after the two years, she will not move. The sea will be atop her, the sea is full of voices, but she will not speak. She will not create the truth, she will not create harmony, she will not move.

This will happen when she dives under the waves and swims down.

When she dives under the seas, all this will end.

She floats on the sea, looking at the sky. She waits for the time she will dive under and dive down.

She waits. She has failed in every moment of her life. She knows there is no sacrifice. She knows there is no harmony, she knows there is no era to come.

She floats on top of the water. We can not die until we are killed by death. The clay flute is on her chest. Birds fly above her, they noise. She makes that same noise in her mouth.

She swims, she is unable to sink. She swims in the direction of flight of birds. She does not notice when her clay flute fell and sank and lay on the bottom of the sea and did not make any further music.

She swam, then she arrived on the bird island. She lay on the sand. She did not call it sand or bird island.

She is asleep. She is asleep.

Her daughters, they called. From the island of Mulatto, from the Briton-named island, from the doomed island, from the island abandoned by WOE, the seven daughters called out. To every island on the earth they called out.

All over the earth, no person listened to the cries of the seven daughters.

All over the earth, nobody was old enough to reach a true age. All over the earth, nobody was young enough to pass through the heart of a mountain.

The world was full of death, also a form of copulation that was a form of death. All over the earth, nobody was old enough to see time clearly. All over the earth, nobody was young enough to be kind.

In the clearings of the doomed island, the

bodies of married men were burnt.

In the rocks of the doomed island, the bodies of married women were burnt.

Unmarried women and girls, they were drowned, their bodies filled the sea.

Unmarried men and boys, they were drowned, their bodies filled the two rivers.

The seven daughters born to WOE, they called out.

Opa walked toward the sunset. She called out: I have no mother, let any man marry me who will.

Twick walked toward the mountain. She called out: I have been silent, and now it is too late.

Glasp walked toward the forest. She called out: Even now I will kill and hurt any one who is my enemy.

Icic walked toward the village. She called out: This pain in my belly, it was with me also before I was born.

Dif walked toward the open temple rocks. She called out: I have tried every belief, and have stopped believing each one.

Test walked toward the eastern river. She called out: I am happy only when no one speaks to me.

Hit walked toward the northern river. She called out: Others have spoken before me, they have spoken better, I do not speak.

The seven walked, they walked away.

They walked through forests, around mountains, past rocks, through rivers. They walked until all had reached the sea.

WOE created the sea. WOE created a boundary. WOE created the sea to stop all persons from walking away forever, to stop all persons from despairing forever, to stop all persons from crying forever.

The seven daughters covered their heads with sand and grieved.

The seven daughters, they are beautiful, no person has seen this beauty. They believe they are ugly. WOE, their mother, she believes they are ugly.

The seven, they called out for their mother.

Fog and smoke and dust fill the throats of the seven.

The seven, they are not eternal.

They will die, WOE.

WOE, you were fated to make seven daughters, no more. But these seven will die.

You will have no daughters. WOE, your island will sink.

WOE, you are not eternal. You are not the god. You are not the name. You are in a body that gives birth, you are in a body that steps across worlds, your body can sink and die, your body will die and your deeds will die.

WOE, your name is forgotten already, you are not WOE, you are nameless.

WOE, your daughters have died to the world, they will be without names, they will even die to you.

WOE, the god within you was she who created. WOE, that god left you after your seventh daughter. You have lost your god.

WOE, an old woman, lies on the sand of the bird island. She created the bird island at the beginning of the universe, but has not seen her creation until this day.

WOE lies on the sand. She has no daughters, she has no friend, she has no father and mother. None will worship her, none will remember her. She has no skill, she has no god, she has no youth, she has no beauty, she has no anger. She has no energizing force, she has no wisdom, she has no enlightenment.

She does not speak the word for birds, she does not speak the word for song, she does not speak the name of the act of singing.

She created an island once, her seven daughters are there.

Somewhere on that island is a clay pot with a clay stopper. Red pigment was kept in the pot. The pot is almost empty now, the pot is stored upside down now.

On the bird island, on a tree on the bird island, an old bird and a young bird are on the same branch.

Young bird beats the air with his wings.

Old bird sits eating the fruit of the tree.

The birds look, each at each. They are confused. They say "How can he do what he does, instead of what I do?"

Bird island is full of song. The old woman hears it. The woman who was WOE hears it.

Song of birds is not the hymn, it is not the word. It is only the song.

WOE hears the song. The old woman hears it. She hears the buo-kota-to, she hears the crow, she hears the magpie, she hears the nightjar, she hears the hoopoe, she hears the tailor bird, she hears the roller bird.

The buo-kota-to, it makes a sound without name. Crows and magpies combine noises that can not be separated. The nightjar is in sound too peculiar, and its name might be evil if spoken. The hoopoe will hoot but WOE does not know that word now. Tailor birds do not know their own names. With harsh screams the roller bird rolls in the air.

WOE who is wise as all deteriorated persons, she lies down among the snakes, she lies down among the scorpions, she sings bird noises she hears, so that when she is bitten by snakes, so that when she is stung by scorpions, she does not say "Oh my hands! Oh my legs!" But she only sings as a bird, because she can sing, she has no pain because she does not sing of pain.

The island will sink, the daughters will die, the mother will die, the winds will cease, the gods will float free. There will be a sunset no one sees. There will be a sunset no one names. There will be a sunset no one describes. There will be a sunset no one remembers. It will be the first sunset. It will be the only sunset.

Birds sing because they can sing. WOE, she sings because she can sing.

WOE listens to songs. She does not capture any songs. She does not keep songs for herself. If a bird flies away, WOE does not follow that bird.

WOE is gone from the island called Mulatto. WOE is gone from the island she thought was the world.

As WOE is gone, the whole of island will sink in the sea.

As WOE is gone, the entire persons of the island will remove out of air, into water.

As WOE is gone, the entire persons of the island will remove out of sunlight, into water.

As WOE is gone, birds are gone, fled off, also no plants are remaining.

What was it to have spoken together?

What was it, to look at faces?

What was it that made faces more than statues, what was it that made persons more than a story?

Persons who told stories, what was it that made the love in those persons, the love of those persons for telling their story, the love in those persons for the story. What was it?

Every mouth will stop telling. The island will be sunken. Women corpses rot in hammocks. Stone crumbles. Sea creatures fall to pieces, sea creatures dry out.

I am WOE, the name. I depart. Forever without being able to listen.

I am WOE, the god. You made a song, just to sing it to me. Your voice went into the world, your voice will never be lost.

I am WOE, the body. You handed me a little gift, it was to eat. I ate it, it lasted forever.

It is not there. Nothing is left from us. Fruit of ten thousand years, all the fruit, nothing.

She who created will not return. She will not create another world all out of her mouth. She will not create another world all about herself. She will not create a world that needs her or knows her. She will withdraw from herself and vanish. She will dive down and disappear. She will float away and imitate birds. She will let go of the rod, she will let go of the stylus, she will let go of the flute. She will forget her name.

The next age of the earth will receive her love from behind the sky. The next age of the earth will receive her love, it will not know her. The next age of the earth is the age without worship. The next age will grow out of the color black.

The island will die, every red berry will become black. Every box-tree will grow roots of air. The wind will blow stone. The night sky will be inverted. Our misdeeds, which put small holes in the sky, will shine through blackly on a white sky.

Wisdom will be in the form of seaweed, it will sink under the water.

All the words that are things, they will hide within things. All the words that are not things, they will degenerate, they will decay, their fibers will come undone, their height will diminish, their breadth will diminish, they will lose their breathing, they will lose their sounding, they will twist apart, they will be eaten by air, they will be turned on their sides, they will be fallen into the sand, they will be hollow, they will be an imprint in the sand, they will be the memory of an imprint.

Every time a man kissed a woman, that will go into the color of the fish in the sea. The fish will not remember.

Every time a girl gave a drink of water to another girl, that will be smoke that does not show against the sky.

The water will not remember the water, the mango will not remember the mango, the rapeseed will not remember the rapeseed, the barking-deer will not remember the barking-deer, the swamp-deer will not remember the swamp-deer, the pangolin will not remember the pangolin, the typhlop will not remember the typhlop, the double-headed snake will not remem-

ber the double-headed snake, the snake-headed
fish will not remember the snake-headed fish, the
white ant will not remember the white ant, the
cuttlefish will not remember the cuttlefish, the
cowrie shell will not remember the cowrie shell,
the glittering mud will not remember the glittering mud, the clay mud will not remember the clay
mud, the man will not remember the man, the
woman will not remember the woman, the corpse
will not remember the corpse, the skeleton will
not remember the skeleton, the memory will not
remember the memory, the island will not remember the island.

Time and illness will be the same. Ambition and the cowrie shell will be the same. Worship and the raindrop will be the same.

The island is completed and gone, the
story will be as a story is before it is told. The
time of the day will be as it is before you are born.
As a dead person is not ill, so the island when
gone will not be in a state of degeneration.

With WOE forgotten, the last word is
spoken, the last god is forgotten, the last names
are forgotten, the last ideas are forgotten, the last
pictures are forgotten, the last songs are forgotten,

the last poems are forgotten, the last stories are
forgotten.

There will be no jokes, only the true form
of jokes. There will be no kindness, only the true
form of kindness. There will be no future, only
the things themselves. There will be no persons,
only the bodies. There will be no happiness, only
an unknown feeling. There will be no souls, but
only depths.

There will be no watcher of things, only
the one. There will be no watched things, only the
one. There will be no watching, only the one.

If I dance, the activity is unknown. If I
dance, the cause is unknown. If I dance, it will not
be called dancing. If I dance, I will not be called
joyful. Dance will have to exist without its name.

When water and earth are unnamed, when
water and earth have lost their names, then they
will join into one place.

The bed of the Swastika opens and
floods the low land with water. Only one hand-
length deep of water, but it is the end. The
people can not bear it.

FLOOD overpowers their minds. A greater flood of FLOOD comes and overpowers them. FLOOD moves heavy blocks of stone out to sea, FLOOD eats grain, it leaves behind mud, FLOOD eats the beloved wife and the blameless children, FLOOD removes the memory of life, FLOOD removes the feeling of calm when you first awaken.

The people stand like funeral carvings. The people are smeared with black dust. Little statues mock the dead by not moving.

The flood takes all names and all words.

The flood leaves nothing for future days.

The flood removes every subject of thinking.

The flood removes every subject of thought.

The name of the flood is "flood," that is the name of FLOOD. Out of a flood is thought to rise fertility.

But FLOOD is infertile, FLOOD is sterile. FLOOD does not speak the name of itself. FLOOD never speaks. FLOOD does not speak one word.

Now the fibers that tie things together, these fibers, the fibers that tie words into sentences, these fibers unwind and split, these fibers rot and snap. The organization of a hut becomes lost in water. The organization of a hut drifts and forgets its order. No sentence can be spoken to put the hut back in order.

Parts of things float every place. Parts of the bodies of men are out of order, afloat. Parts of the island turn slowly, trees float away from each other. Stones move by themselves, they go the direction of stones, they go by the will of stones. No sentence can organize this, the gods are in pieces, parts of things have no entire god. No god is able to speak. Only FLOOD, who will not.

Now the flood returns to its river. All its water is new, it is not the same river as before. The flood draws back. The island is in the sunlight. The island is in the air.

Where there were huts, there are stones.

Where there were persons, fish die.

The earth has no energy in its feet, the earth has no power in its eyes, the earth has no procreative force, the earth has no wit in its mind, the earth has no breath in its center, the earth has no tongue in its mouth.

The eighth daughter of WOE, the unborn daughter, the daughter who is not named, she is not drowned. She has no body, she has no name.

The eighth daughter of WOE, she cries out. She looks at the death of the island, she cries out. She looks at the death of TIME, she cries out. She looks at the throat of FLOOD, she cries out.

She calls to her mother and she calls to her sisters.

She calls to her mother by her name, WOE.

WOE is now named. WOE is to be seen, WOE is on the flooded island, WOE is on the dead island, she walks here, she is named so that she walks where life walked. She walks here.

WOE looks. She remembers the persons of this island, she sees the persons of this island.

WOE sees persons, alive. She sees the persons of the island play a game with a pink ball.

They never want to stop playing.

Each person plays with the pink ball that floats slowly upward.

Each person who plays, he wins, and no person loses the game.

Each player praises himself. In this playing, their time is lost. In this playing, their hours are lost. In this playing, their days are lost.

WOE picks up a pink ball at her feet.

WOE plays all day the game with the pink ball that floats slowly upward.

Her seven daughters who were born, they can watch, they can see. They are here to watch, they can see.

The seven daughters cry out. They bitterly

criticize the game. Their bitterness makes the pink ball fall to the ground, it has fallen to the ground, it is covered with dust.

The seven cry bitterly: Will we never be born again?

WOE walks on the ground, she picks up the pink ball from the ground, praising herself and making the retrieval of the ball into a story.

Then she plays with the others, her friends, her fellow citizens, the ones she shares history with, the ones she shares fables with, the ones who have sung hymns to her, the ones who understand her, her compatriots, her companions.

She throws the ball and says: My friends understand me.

The ball floats, it floats upward, she praises herself, and her friends praise themselves.

The seven daughters of WOE weep, the seven daughters shout: Our sister should be born! Your eighth daughter, she should be born! She who can free us, she should be born! Your daughter who is not yet born, she should be born! Your final daughter, she should be born!

WOE replies: She will not be born. The girl without a name will not ever be born.

The eighth daughter of WOE also answers her sisters, she speaks, she answers and says:

I could not be born. So that I determined to be born as a statue. So that I could continually speak one word. I would continually speak the word of "word." I would sink and settle at the sea bottom, and speak for ever.

However this birthing as a statue did not complete. I could not be born.

I determined to be born as a burrowing mole or underground type of rat. I spoke the names for beast, while digging and covering myself with dirt. This dirt was warm, I felt of the mole, I felt the skin of a mole, I had the breath of a mole. I felt then to crawl away and undermine and become a secret. But I then felt the word for light, I felt the warmth of the name of light.

At that time I said I must be born as a river, I was the river. I flowed into the mountain,

I flowed up out of the mountain. I was a river who could almost stop its moving. I was a river who could be dry water. I was a river who could be silent and torrent at the same time.

I was a river who could flow in a circle. I flowed in a circle and grew pain. I rose and flooded over, I flooded, I flooded the whole world. I flowed out of the circle, I flowed into the sea, I felt less of pain then.

I thereby flowed into the whole sea. I flowed away entirely. What came after me was new water, fresh water, that was the meaning of fresh water, I was not any of myself. I was the river but I was gone. I was the river, I was going to die each day. I was unkillable, I was the river who does not remember.

That is what the unborn daughter said.

WOE then replied to her daughters, to her seven daughters and to her eighth daughter:

I do not know my eighth daughter.

I can not speak to my eighth daughter.

My eighth daughter is confused in my mind. I do not love her.

I do not wish to love my eighth daughter.

It is difficult having more and more daughters, more and more daughters.

It is time for the seven of you to die.

Persons do not live forever. You have done nothing worthy, yet you have lived since before Magellan.

Now the world is at an end.

There is no world for you to be born into. There is no world for you to walk. There is no world for you to sleep in. There is no world for you to speak in. There is no world.

There is no living world. There is no other world or different world. There is no world for you. There is no world.

That is what WOE said.

The seven daughters of WOE, they fell

into the dust, they threw themselves down in the dust, at the place where the pink ball is played with by all the islanders except themselves.

The seven daughters lie in the dust, and the gods of speech are insulted and flee them. The light fails for them. Dust itself will not cushion them, the dust wounds their bodies. They do not weep, the daughters do not know how to weep, because WEEP has left them.

They can see nobody living on the entire island except for their mother. They see the corpses in the water of the two rivers. They see the corpses of men and women and dogs and girls and all animals of all type. They see the broken huts and killed trees. They see their mother alone, playing with a pink ball.

WOE loved each of the seven. WOE beat them each when she felt angry. WOE lost her remembrance of how to be a mother. WOE tried to forget she had seven daughters. WOE stopped trying to have an eighth daughter. WOE successfully failed to have an eighth daughter.

If WOE forgot her seven daughters, they would not be here on this island. WOE has not successfully forgotten her daughters. But she will not speak to them. She will not see them.

WOE once said: My daughters are my deed, no matter what the world says about them.

Now she does not speak to her daughters, she does not see them.

They call her name, saying Mother, they call her name, saying WOE.

She remembers them and says: I regret I wasted my time. I could have been playing with this ball, for those many years. I could have enjoyed my friends, for those many years. Instead I sat in a hut with you seven, and I was lonely.

That is what WOE says. The hearts of the seven are in pain.

They lie in the dust for nine days. Then they arise and walk to the mountain.

The first daughter runs. The first daughter runs at the mountain, heedless.

The second daughter bows her head. The

second daughter bows her head, praying, to approach the mountain she bows her head praying.

The third daughter attacks. The third daughter attacks the mountain by throwing stones at it.

The fourth daughter looks. The fourth daughter looks at herself in a bronze mirror, with the mountain over her shoulder, also in the mirror.

The fifth daughter sings. The fifth daughter sings to the mountain, she sings love songs to the mountain, she sings.

The sixth daughter walks. The sixth daughter walks to the foot of the mountain, she is thunder, she batters the mountain with sound.

The seventh daughter is atop. The seventh daughter is already atop the mountain. The seventh daughter is looking out at the entire world.

She is very weak. The seventh daughter, she is thin and weak. It is her fate to find the eighth daughter. She reads the fragments, written in stones at the top of the mountain.

The fragments of her sister, the fragments of the eighth daughter, they are written in signs no one can speak.

The fragments are broken, they are fragments. The hair of the eighth daughter. The arm of the eighth daughter. The foot of the eighth daughter.

The parts of a girl are not a girl who can move or live.

She is dead because unborn, unwritten and unthought.

For many years WOE played with the pink ball all along the beach, but her eyes did not see the dead bodies of islanders washing ashore.

WOE played with the pink ball beside the cooking-place, but her eyes did not see the bodies burning in stacks.

WOE played with the pink ball along the copper-colored river, but her eyes did not see the bodies blocking the water, entangling the water of the river.

WOE played with the pink ball, throwing it high, but her eyes did not see the smoke of the burning persons.

WOE played with the pink ball, throwing it low, but her eyes did not see the pits of bodies of persons she once knew.

WOE played with the pink ball, throwing it to her friends, she could see all the islanders and they were willing to play with her, they hugged and praised her.

Although she knew they were all dead, burning in stacks and floating in rivers etc., she played with the pink ball and said: They have all gone to sleep! They will all awaken!

On one day WOE rubs her eyes. The world is silent, her seven daughters have left her, they have gone to the mountain, they have gone away in the seven directions, they have gone to seek some thing.

I have gone to sleep, says WOE.

I have lost my daughters!

She speaks their names, she speaks:

Opa

Twick

Glasp

Icic

Dif

Test

Hit

In the past, she kept them alive. This is how she kept them alive longer than woman years, longer than person years: she spoke their names, when no one else did.

When she would speak their names, they would appear. She would think of them and they would appear.

Now she speaks the seven names. But she

speaks as if she is talking to other persons.

She does not think of the seven living girls as she speaks: she thinks of her friends, she thinks of the game.

She speaks the true names of her daughters to her friends, her friends who praise her. To those friends WOE speaks the true names of her only daughters.

Her daughters do not appear. She does not see them appear. They do not come to her, and she is alone of them.

1160
1020
951
947
921
900

/

Made in the USA
Charleston, SC
02 November 2010